SEVEN DAYS TO SAY GOODBYE

SEVEN DAYS TO SAY GOODBYE

Dawn Michele

iUniverse, Inc.
New York Lincoln Shanghai

Seven Days To Say Goodbye

iUniverse books may be ordered through booksellers or by contacting:

iUniverse
2021 Pine Lake Road, Suite 100
Lincoln, NE 68512
www.iuniverse.com
1-800-Authors (1-800-288-4677)

ISBN-13: 978-0-595-39127-1 (pbk)
ISBN-13: 978-0-595-83513-3 (ebk)
ISBN-10: 0-595-39127-3 (pbk)
ISBN-10: 0-595-83513-9 (cbk)

Printed in the United States of America

For Joie Lynne
1971–1990

www.pomc.com

I guess that all we have is now. There aren't any reasons good enough, to delay the emotions we feel at this very moment. It took Joie's untimely death to shake me into that reality. I have traveled to so many places in our childhood since she left. There isn't one place I can go and not find her there. That's something that stays with you forever. You only realize it when you have to go back and rely on just the past to get you through. My pain is real and my heart is finally mending.

But just like in a classic fantasy, I can't help but wonder what she'd be doing if she were still here in my life. How many kids would she have and how many times would I have babysat them? I go to the cemetery for peace and some sort of closure that eludes me for just that very moment. I talk to her there. She hears me and all of my crazy thoughts. I can honestly say, that I would give anything to have the chance to say, "I love you" and "Goodbye".

Joie was the beauty and I was the brain. Somehow it just worked out that way. Even in the 9th grade, she still hadn't memorized our home telephone number. It just wasn't a priority with her. But she could tell you every single eligible freshman in High School. Yeah, that's what she knew best. The only other thing she knew better was the art of dancing. She could make up a ballet to "Mary Had A Little Lamb". God gave her that incredible gift of rhythm. She took full advantage of it.

Looking back, those dances in the basement to the jukebox, are such classic examples of what could have been. But she was taken too soon. Joie died at the hands of another. Someone she knew in fact. How do you explain that to a 6-year-old little brother that was her whole world? I was 21 when she died and he was just 6.

Children at that age never know fear, because of their child-like faith. Now that faith was abruptly replaced by fear. The fear of not knowing why Joie was never coming back to see him. The fear that whoever got her might get him. It all intertwines.

As the years have passed, I have found my solace in music. God gave me that gift at an older age. I was 13 when I discovered my abilities for music. Not knowing then what he had in store for me. Hindsight is always 20/20. He gave me the gift of music to help and heal others' pain. And I know in a lot of ways I have accomplished just that.

But I cannot put myself in the present tense of any of my music. I write of others' stories and their journey of mourning. Not mine. But hearing some of their thoughts and struggles really puts mine into that place in the soul where it can never be touched or understood by anyone. Not even myself.

To heal from such a tragedy, one must let complete devastation in. I never did that until I met Sam. Sam is an Angel. He was great. He was sent to help me overcome a bigger suffering than the one I thought I was going through.

I guess now, my loss isn't my biggest fear, nor is it my deepest sorrow. I am at this moment left wondering what God is going to do with the rest of my eternity.

Maybe I should have never let Sam come into my life and give me such a great offer. He came out of nowhere while I was at the cemetery and heard one of my many conversations with Joie. I guess I should tell you what happened with Joie so that you can understand why Sam offered me the gift of a "Second Chance".

Joie was murdered in December of 1990 at the age of 19. Too young to know what she wanted from her future and to naïve to be living in the present. I guess for her, there was no way out. Joie was on the East Coast living with her best friend and soul mate, Erin. Erin loved my sister with an unconditional love that proved to be one of the few happiest experiences in my sisters conflicted life.

To make this story more understandable, I need to say that Joie was the type to help anyone and everyone. Including animals. Needless to say, when Erin was being abused by her boyfriend Michael, Joie was the one to take her in and give her refuge from this young man who tried to overtake every aspect of Erin's life.

It was Joie's thoughtless act of charity that ultimately cost her, her life. Michael killed Joie in an attempt to get Erin back. I don't know what makes a man so angry that he overpowers any woman and takes away the ultimate freedom in this life; that being…Living……

Michael took Joie from all of us and from this world. I can't imagine what my mother and father must feel like. They were the ones to give her life, and I know without a doubt, that they never planned to outlive her, or any of us kids for that matter. Needless to say, Sam came along at just the right time and with what I thought, was just the right offer.

The reason I believe that, is because I have spent many months and years wishing I could go back in time and have the opportunity to hold her again, and ultimately say goodbye. Because, she left all of us without saying goodbye. That leaves a hole inside of your heart that can't be measured, let alone be justified. There is no "trial" or "test" harder than trying to understand the death of your sibling or child. It's something you work on your whole life, yet never find all the answers to, so that you can pass the test. It just doesn't happen. There isn't a greater pain than losing someone you love.

Especially in the case of a murder.

Not to minimize someone who loses their life to a deadly illness, but at least there is time to prepare and say some good-byes. But suicide and murder do not give you that chance to say goodbye. I wish they did, because I would have never let Sam tell me of a way to mend my heart. It was great when I first heard the idea, but I paid and am still paying the ultimate price for my decision to take him up on it.

You see, Sam offered me the chance to go back seven days before Joie's death and be with her and her surroundings. Sam was tall and stood even taller as a Heavenly Being, in my opinion. His face was easy to remember: especially when I saw him for the first time. Sam had so much happiness about him that it made me believe his words were chosen specifically for me. I was drawn to his light immediately.

Where would he stay if I went back in time? Would Joie know anything about my journey and how far I had come? So many reasons to go…

My motives were to tell her that I loved her and give her the best seven days I could give her. What I wasn't prepared for, were the stipulations that Sam put in the deal. He would send me back, but the kicker was that I would know everything I knew right now, and couldn't change history.

With that knowledge, why wouldn't I want to change it? Especially if it meant that she would still be here and an everyday part of our family? He said that I could spend every moment I could in seven days, but that on the day of her death, I could not warn her nor divert what had already happened, because changing the future affects more than just her and I.

Because of my longing to be with her one last time, I quickly agreed to all of his terms and conditions. He warned me that my eternity would forever be changed if I interfered. I knew that it would be hard, but that it was possible to overcome the feeling of wanting to save her from the hands of evil.

I did ask Sam if taking her place was an option, and of course, that was thrown out immediately. He just wanted to give me the chance that thousands before me had longed for, but never could do, because of ulterior motives. I don't know. Joie was so special to our family, and like I said, I jumped at the chance to be with her just one last time. Hey, seven days was a long time frame to be with her, and when the final day arrived, I figured that it would be okay to let history become many people's future. That was then…This is definitely NOW…

Day 1

I woke up in Maryland in Joie's apartment to the sound of her yelling at me to get out of bed. Huh? She ran in and asked if I was going to sleep all day. My dream had become a reality. I was with her and we were together. Time had somehow rewound itself. Or had it? Sam really sent me back. And that meant that I had a lot of agreements and promises to keep.

Joie looked as beautiful as I had remembered. Her hair was long and curly with a very subtle hint of red in it…She had always looked like Molly Ringwald with that hairstyle. Her lips were glazed in the latest flavor of gloss. Her nails were freshly painted and she was as short as ever. Yeah, she was all of five foot nothing…I found myself following her every move across the room, until she came into the kitchen.

Joie said that she would be back in a while because her photo shoot wouldn't take long. I quickly jumped out of bed and threw a cap on my head to accompany her to her appointment. She didn't seem to mind as much as she wondered why in the world I had had an actual interest in her modeling. We caught a cab (after walking a block in the frozen tundra) and I just absorbed everything. She very quickly noticed me staring at her and asked me to "take a picture, they last longer!".

I must have been in a daze, because she had already asked me three times. I only apologized and tried making sense of my surroundings and of her. In my mind, the clock was ticking. But where was Sam? Was he going to ever show himself to me in the coming days? I wanted to ask him so many things. I guess I would just have to ask him when he brought me back to my reality not hers. Joie was as beautiful as I remembered. It was wonderful to hear her voice, even if she was yelling at the taxicab driver. It was Joie and we were together. I asked her for a hug and she asked me to drop dead. (I assumed by that, that she had no idea how far I had come and that she had no idea of what ultimately lie ahead for her and our family.)

We got to the first of a couple photo shoots that week and met a few of her friends who were scheduled to help with her hair and make-up that day. Erin quickly greeted me and a million thoughts began racing through my mind. Erin was Joie's best friend and in my hindsight was possibly the true essence of what I would have left of Joie in my future, except my memories.

Erin was taller than Joie and had some unnatural highlights in her hair as well. She was a brunette by nature and a blonde by night. She had brown eyes and a very loving smile. Erin was a very attractive young lady just like her counterpart, Joie Lynne. The two of them were more beautiful than the Seven Wonders combined.

Erin asked me how much fun I'd been having since I'd arrived, and I quickly thought about how much fun I wanted to make Joie's last week. What a closed question, I thought. I told Erin that I wanted to make every second count. She just said, that she and Joie would show me a great time. And I really counted on that. It was beginning to feel alot like Christmas again, and I couldn't wait to share a part of that with her.

Even if it was for just seven days.

During the photo shoot, I found myself staring at Joie so as to memorize each smile and glimmer in her eyes. The funniest part was when the photographer had a few extra shots left and asked me to join in on them. Joie quickly retorted by telling him that she couldn't believe he was asking us to pose for one shot because it only cemented the fact that we were characters from the Adamms Family. How could I resist...I quickly whispered something in his ear and within a few seconds, I shouted "Now!" and he took it just as kissed her for the shot. And what a shot...I don't know who was more shocked, her or me...To my surprise, she looked around the room and found a small stool and quickly grabbed it and THREW it at me...Yeah, the photographer got that one too.

That was Joie, she couldn't fight or defend herself, but she could throw anything at anyone and at anytime. I thought back for a moment to the time when she broke my arm from throwing a can of green beans at me because I wouldn't give her the toilet I was sitting on.

Let's not forget that there were THREE other bathrooms in the house…And I was the one who got grounded for not being the "mature" one and giving up my seat…Such hard times. I laugh instinctively now at the very thought of all those instances.

We got done with the photo shoot and the photographer said to come back and see him the following Monday, December 4…Joie noted that without a doubt she would be there and he better be ready…As I listened to their conversation, I knew that none of that would happen because Joie's death was on Sunday, December 3. Unless I could find a way to stop it all. But what would Sam do to me? I guess you don't cross an Angel. But I sure wanted to try.

We left with Erin and got some lunch at a seafood place. Let me tell you how much I hate seafood…Joie lived on it, and it sure looked like I was going to starve to death if we kept eating it. I looked at my watch and realized that it was actually dinnertime and not lunchtime. Joie and Erin told me that now that I was here, I would have to keep their schedule. And since they had just woke up a few hours earlier, it was only breakfast. I asked Joie if we could just sit and talk. She asked me why, and I just said because I missed her.

As Joie talked, I listened. I immersed myself in hearing her voice and trying to memorize it. I thought about the future I had come from and how hard it had been after several years of not hearing from her. Even then, I still had to play a video just to remember what she sounded like. I have many memories inside my mind, but the voice recalling them is always the same…Mine…

We talked about her life and mine and things that finally mattered to her. She was growing up. This was a comfort to know. My baby sister actually had feelings of true love for her family and friends.

I asked Joie if she was truly happy in her life right now. She told me that things were always ok, but could be better.

Joie chose a far different path than me. Actually, a far different path than a lot of people. She made choices that ultimately affected every aspect of everyone's life. Death will do that to anyone at anytime.

Joie sat and told me what she really wanted from life, and I cringed at the very thought of nothing being further from the truth. In my silence, which Joie sensed, she asked me what I was so worried about. I tried to make up some story about a music theory class I was in back in college at the time, but she didn't buy it.

Joie and I had a great talk that day, and I wanted so much to tell her to run, and never look back, so that she would be home when I got back on Sunday. But I could still hear Sam telling me that I wasn't allowed that privilege. How do you honor an Angel and still get what you want by saving the day? That remained to be seen.

The phone rang as Joie and I talked. As a matter of fact, the phone rang non-stop. Everyone loved her and needed her for this or for that. Photo-ops or practicing dance routines. You name it, she could do it. Well, except sing. There wasn't one ounce of musical talent in her body. I am still amazed at her determination to be the lead singer of her own band. Laughable. Absolutely laughable.

As Joie got up to answer the phone, Erin was in the kitchen and grabbed it first. I heard Erin ask several times "Hello?" but they didn't say anything. Erin said some rather abrasive words and slammed the phone down.

"Who was that?" I asked…

"Oh, it's 'The Caller'" Erin said.

Joie chimed in about all of these prank phone calls they had been getting from a "sicko". Joie said that they had been to the police, but that they couldn't do anything about it unless he threatened them.

"Do you know who would do this to you?"

Joie said it was probably one of her many admirers from the club where she danced at. I told her that wasn't even funny.

"Well I do have admirers, you know!" she said.

I started for the kitchen and asked the both of them if they were the least bit worried. Erin said that he had been calling for a couple of months now and really was no harm, so why worry about it. Joie said she just toyed with him whenever she was the one to answer the phone. As I sat there listening to them talk about him, I really couldn't wait for my turn to answer it.

We left about 10:30 to head to the club where Joie worked. This would be an experience in itself. I have never been in a place like that, but she wanted to show me where she worked and to meet some of her friends.

As we got in the door to "Memories", people started coming up to her immediately. She introduced me as her "goody-two shoes" sister and I made every effort to "hear" each name as they were introduced above the loud music. Joie found a booth and asked me to wait in it. I happily obliged.

As soon as they left to go meet their friends, Sam sat down.

"Where have you been?" I asked.

"How was your first day" he countered.

I told him of the days events and he said that that was why he was here. He told me that I had already started changing the future including mine.

"What? What do you mean?"

He reminded me of the photo shoot earlier that day.

"So what does that have to do with changing the future, and why is that a problem".

He explained that in the first investigation, the photographer was questioned and I was never mentioned. Now in the future, I was listed as someone who was in her very last photos. I started to sweat. Sam told me to not involve myself in anything else.

"You didn't give me a list of rules to follow, so anything is fair game" I snapped.

He calmly reminded me that my seven days here were a gift and to use them wisely.

"Well, if you're not around to tell me what I can and can't do, then how will I know what affects the future of my family?"

"I'll be here Dawn, but you're the only one who will know it. Take my advice and just enjoy her company and say those things you told me you wanted to say. I am warning you now, that you cannot change what has happened. It can't be done. God will surely punish you if you take away the agency of someone else. Don't do it Dawn."

And with that, he was gone.

Joie and Erin walked up to the table and asked if I was going to sit there all night. I asked them what time it was. It was after 1am.

"I'm tired, when are we leaving?"

"You're not serious are you" Joie asked.

"Listen Dawn, when we go out, it's all night long." I was stuck in a continuous party, I thought.

Well, about 4 am, we finally got home and I have never been so happy to see a pillow.

Day 2

Music was created so that one can appreciate it, not distort it. Joie and Erin had the radio so loud that I could barely hear my head pound. As I lay there on the couch, the two of them screamed the words to the song at the top of their lungs. I was actually glad for volume control, so as to drown out their inability to carry a tune. And why couldn't they play a little Christmas music? Why did it have to be hard rock? The phone rang again, and Joie answered it.

It was no surprise that "The Caller" wasn't saying anything. Who was he? Joie flirted with him effortlessly. I sat and listened. When she finally hung up on him, I tried to caution her about who she said those kinds of things to. She told me not to worry because Erin and her had been doing this everyday and it seemed harmless.

"Why do you even bother talking to him?" I said.

"We think it's fun!" Joie replied.

"Don't you wonder who's on the other end? I mean, come on, he could be a serial killer and you two are leading him on" I retorted.

She only continued to make jokes about the whole issue. It was only a few moments later when the very next song on the radio was a song called "Joey" by Concrete Blonde. This actually pushed me back to the present day from which I had come.

In 1990 when that song had originally come out, Joie called me on the phone and was so excited because she said it was "totally about her"…At that point in time, I truly agreed. Knowing what I know now, I have listened to that song to help mend my broken heart and to understand what she must have gone through. Now being back in time with her, it was weird to hear it on the radio as a "brand new song" for the group and even stranger to have her be so excited to hear it again. So many memories surfaced because of that song.

And I could never tell Joie any of it.

As the song played, I closed my eyes and remembered. I also cringed as Joie belted out each note off key at the top of her lungs. Poor rockstar; never gonna find an off key rock band. She asked me very boldly when the song was over, if I would be her "keyboardist" in her band.

How hard can I laugh?

Well, at that moment, I could have peed my pants from laughter. She wondered what was so funny. I asked "Who is going to be the lead singer?"…

"Well, who do you think" she quipped.

"You?" I shouted as I choked on my saliva…

"And why not?" she retorted.

I shrugged my shoulders and kindly stated "Your talent is dancing, not singing".

She took her little dancing self into the kitchen and found the biggest Tupperware Bowl she could find and chucked it at me. I can't tell you how many times I have ducked in my life from a flying object she has thrown.

One time when we were teenagers, (and our mother had just started dating our future Step-father), he taught us the valuable virtue of patience and counting to ten. He had just brought over his hand carved and hand painted chess set and was teaching me how to play. Joie and I got into one of our before you knew it, Joie ran to the kitchen and grabbed a frying pan lid. Without hesitation, she threw it like a frisbee at my head, and of course, I ducked: only to hear the shattering of ceramic kings and queens from behind me. Yep, Pete's beautiful chess set was gone in the blink of an eye, and all his little men could not be put back together again.

As we both stood there in silence and wondered who Pete was going to kill first, we both pointed fingers at the other one. And as usual, I got grounded because I was the older one and should have been more "mature" and let Joie have her way. Yeah right.

As the Tupperware bowl flew by me, I picked it up and ran after her. She started to run because she knew I could catch her and pulverize her down to nothing. As I caught up to her and pushed her to the ground, she started flailing her arms around and kicking and screaming and laughing. Yeah, what a beautiful sight. We were laughing together and her eyes had life in them again. As I raised my hands to "give" her back the Tupperware bowl, I just started laughing.

"You're so cute Joie!!"

She looked at me and said to get off of her and quit acting so strange. I guess to her, any amount of sincerity from any of her siblings would seem "strange" to her. But if she only knew how far I had come, then maybe she'd lighten up.

I asked Joie what was on the agenda for today. She said that we were going to go shopping for clothes (my least favorite thing to do) and then catch a movie. I asked them if we could go see "Ghost". Joie and Erin both seemed intrigued by the horror films instead of the love stories.

That movie was so encompassing to me for so many different reasons. It was a movie that I had watched over and over just to not miss her so much when she had passed away. And if I could just get her to watch it with me, I could take that one moment back with me on Sunday.

I can't believe that I just said that word.

Sunday.

That was going to be the day that I wished could stand still. I dreaded that day now. Sunday has always been a day of rest for me and my family, and now it would be a day of tests. How ironic. This was a test I hoped to flunk. I wish that Sam were here, so that I could figure out something.

We got in a cab and headed for the mall to do some Christmas shopping. I immediately wanted to head for the food court and Joie and Erin wanted to find some new clothes for work. As Joie and Erin headed for the lingerie shop, I set my sights on feeding my guts. As I walked through the mall looking for a place to eat, I came across an older toy store. I decided to see what they had on the shelves to see if I could find anything nostalgic for Joie as a Christmas present.

On the second aisle of the toy store I came across "Lincoln Logs". Wow!! It reminded me of all the Friday nights Joie and I spent with our dad and step-mom Elise on their weekends to have us. Joie and I played with Lincoln Logs well into our teens. Back in the day, we only had TinkerToys and Lincoln Logs. Every weekend when we arrived at our dad and Elise's, we always had the same routine. On Friday it was Lincoln Logs, The Dukes of Hazard (them good ol' boys) and we ended the weekend with Donny and Marie. (You remember that show don't you?)

I turned down the next aisle…GAMES!! Sometimes we played COOTIE on Saturday nights. Yahtzee was Elise's favorite game: and it taught Joie and I how to add and subtract.

As I walked further down the aisle, I came across "Mr. PotatoHead". "Hey Mr. PotatoHead, where have you been hiding out?" Of course he didn't answer: but I picked him up and kept talking to him anyway. I put his eyes and ears and mouth on and I proceeded to ask him what I was going to do on Sunday. Maybe he would have an answer. As the minutes passed, his silence echoed in my mind. "Do nothing," was his silent reply. That was not the answer I had hoped for. I put him back on the shelf and continued to browse.

After a couple more minutes of looking around, I went back and bought the Lincoln Logs because of the symbolic meaning to Joie and I. The cashier asked me who the Lincoln Logs were for.

"For your niece? Or nephew?"

"Nope! It's for my 19 year old sister! I wanted something nostalgic from our childhood. And she and I have built more houses with Lincoln Logs than any construction company I know". And with that, I left his wonderful store.

As I continued to look for the food court, I noticed a security guard talking to Joie and Erin. I quickly ran up to them and asked if everything was ok. Erin seemed quite upset and Joie was doing all the talking to the security guard and giving him their personal information.

That was very odd in itself, since Joie can't remember her own address, social security number or home phone number for that matter. I chuckled inside myself.

Erin tried to tell me that Michael had just spotted them in the mall and kept harassing the both of them. He finally threatened Erin and told her that if she didn't come back to him, he'd take care of her "one way or another". Some things were finally starting to make sense. I had remembered from the murder trial that Michael had threatened Erin several times, that he would kill her and her lover is she ever left him.

Michael and Erin had been together for several years, and the relationship went extremely downhill over that last several months. In fact it had been unhealthy almost from the beginning.

Michael was tall, with dark long hair (not how I had seen him at the trial) and unshaven. A sight that did not appeal to me in every way possible. His face seemed aged from the hard lifestyle he was living. He looked mean. And I say that truthfully, not because of what he did, but because of how he came across…

Erin was afraid to leave him in the beginning. I guess I would have been as well…He stood about 6 ft 1 and outweighed her by at least 100 lbs.

In the courtroom, for the murder trial, he appeared before the jury clean shaven and short hair. You would have never thought him to look like a druggie. He looked sharp in his new suit, like he was on his lunch break from Wall Street.

He was obsessed, to say the least. But with Joie as her "body guard", the two of them, Erin and Joie, seemed unstoppable. Well, at least they were legends in their own minds. Brings a smile to my face in that regard. When I looked at Michael, he reminded me of Pee Wee Herman…Not a very attractive sight, right? Michael cared not, that Erin and Joie were talking to the police. Erin reiterrated what Michael had screamed at her…"If you leave me…"

So of course Joie had heard all of this and had taken matters into her own hands and told Erin "You don't have to take that from him; you can stay with me for as long as you want until you get on your feet!" And because of that statement, Erin moved in. Joie never thought with her head, always her heart. That's why so many people felt a void in their lives on Dec. 3, 1990.

As Joie tried to calm Erin down and reassure her that Michael couldn't hurt her, she noticed my bag from the toystore.

"What's that?" she asked inquisitively. "Is it for Brian for Christmas?"

"Nope, guess again!" I countered.

"Josh? Kelli? Brandi?" in her unsure voice.

"Not even close" I said.

As I watched her try and figure out who it was for, her eyes were eluding to the fact that she had run out of choices. Before she burned up the rest of her brain cells over such and easy question, I quickly announced: "It's for you!"…

"Me? Well what is it?" she asked as she tried to grab it from my hand.

"Uh-uh-ahh" I said as I shook my index finger from left to right. "You have to wait until Christmas!" I said.

"That's not fair; I'd tell you what I had if I had something." She countered.

"Well, I would wait until Christmas," I concluded. "Which brings me to my next question; What DID you get me for Christmas?"

"You'll just have to wait until Christmas" she recounted as she mimicked my answer.

"Actually Dawn, I ordered your present a few weeks ago and it should be here anyday now" Joie said without any hesitation.

"Well there's no telling what it is, knowing your demented thinking" I teased.

"I think you'll really like it, just ask Erin" she said.

I looked at Erin for some sign of acknowledgement to Joie's statement. Erin quickly agreed with Joie, "Dawn you're crazy for liking this sort of thing—but Joie really did want this to be a great Christmas for you to remember. So trust me, you'll love it."

As we started to leave the mall, we walked past the movie theateres and I begged Joie and Erin to see "Ghost" with me.

"It starts in 15 minutes you guys-please."

Erin turned to Joie "Come on Jo—it can't be that bad." And before I had to beg even another second, we went in to the movie; and although she didn't know it, Joie started to heal me.

As we watched, Joie got teary-eyed from time to time, and laughed at everything Whoopi Goldberg said. Whoopi/Oda Mae sure helped me laugh a lot during those original dark days in 1990.

I really want to thank her for that. Thanks Whoopi—for choosing to play a character that so many people can relate to no matter when they watch your movie "Ghost".

At the end of the movie we got into the cab to go home, and I started to question Joie about her thoughts and feelings over what she had just seen. The solemn look on her face led me to believe that she was in very deep contemplation.

"What's on your mind Hasbro?" I asked.

"I was just thinking about some things." She said quietly.

"Oh, yeah, like what?" I asked

"Well (she paused) I'm not afraid to die:" she said calmly.

"What?" I said.

"Well, when you die, your brain produces endorphins so that you don't feel the pain: the only thing that would hurt me about dying is that I would never want to leave mom." She turned to Erin and said "You promise me, that if anything ever happens to me, you'll make sure that my mom knows that I loved her more."

Erin got serious for just a moment and said "Of course I would, but don't you talk like that; you're not going anywhere."

Joie just sat there silently.

Finally I broke the silence by striking up the exact same conversation we had had on the phone on the Tuesday before she died. She had called me in Utah where I was attending college. Trying to recall her words that day came so easily.

"You know Joie, I know you're young and 'living it up'—but in the eternal scheme of things, are you truly happy?"

(It was about this time when the cab driver started flipping through the radio stations…)

"Some days I am, but most days it's hard," she said sadly. "I keep doing what all my friends are doing."

I pushed her for a more finite answer. "I think you miss all those things that are so important to you, like family and church, don't you?"

"I do Dawn, but I don't know if I'm ready to change," she admitted.

"You don't have to change everything all at once; just pick a few things to work on and start with that. I can help you if you need anything", I reaffirmed to her.

"I've been doing these things for so long now, that I've forgotten how to be the real me," she stated with sadness.

She turned her head to the song on the radio…

"Well Joie, you know what's right and wrong, and you never know when you're going to go, so I think you should get your life in order so that you won't have any regrets. Just like my friend Kim. She died in a car wreck on her way home from college last year. I went to her funeral and listened to everything that she had accomplished in her short 19 years—and realized that she had lived and done more in her young life than alot of people will ever do in their entire lives. You don't want regrets Joie. Just do what you know is right and Heavenly Father will provide a way for the rest. I promise."

She listened intensely to me and said "I'm just not ready Dawn, but I'm think-ing about some things." And with those words, she turned the conversation to Erin and their photo shoot tomorrow.

My stomach got a pit because Elton John's "Tiny Dancer" came on the radio. I hadn't ever really paid attention to that song until after Joie had died. And it had played a pivotal role in my memories of her…

For the last 15 years, I would always turn that song up even louder just to be closer to her. And now she was with me, "always with me, Tiny Dancer in my hand". My Tiny Dancer was in the cab. And had no idea of how deeply I had been moved…All she could talk about was…

"Which shoes do you think I should wear tomorrow?" Joie clammered.

Erin eagerly said, "I think you should wear your black fish-net heels: they will match all of your outfits."

"I was thinking that too! I just have to find my right heel though—I think Holly snatched it and hid it from me." she said.

I had forgotten about Holly.

Actually "Hollywood" was her real name.

Although for a rottweiler, that was a gentle name.

Joie and her (now) ex-boyfriend Eric had gotten her as a puppy while they were on vacation in Hollywood, California in the summer of '89. Joie had also visited our Nana & Tata and other family members in California, then jumped across the state line to Arizona to visit my Dad, Elise, Josh, Kelli and Brian for what would be (unbeknownst to them) the last time in her life.

"Hey Joie, where is Holly?" I asked.

"Eric has her this week." She saw the confused look on my face. "When we broke up, we both wanted custody of her, so we settled on joint custody" she answered.

"Are you serious?" I laughed.

"It's not funny! I miss her when she's gone" she answered in defense. "She's our baby. We both love her."

"When is she coming back" I asked, (hoping it would be Saturday or Sunday)

"Probably not until Monday—because Erin and I go out on Sunday and I won't be home until after that."

Now my mind was really racing. I remember several people (including Eric) telling my mother that if Holly had been in the apartment that Sunday night, then Michael would have never succeeded in hurting Joie in any way.

"That's it!" I thought, "All I have to do is get Eric's phone number and tell him to bring Holly home so I can visit her too."

As my thoughts turned into a small plan to save Joie, we pulled into their apartment complex. As we entered the 'secured gates', I noticed how easily we passed through them.

"Joie" I said, "How come those security gates let us through with out any kind of key or buzzer of any kind?"

"Oh these gates have been broken so long, and they won't fix them: I've asked many times" she answered.

"Well anyone can get through them; that's not right!" I exclaimed.

Erin interrupted, "Believe me, we wish they would fix these gates. We're paying for secured apartment living that we aren't getting."

"You should call the police to come here and make your apartment managers fix all of the broken gates. Anyone can get in here at anytime" I replied.

Joie seemed like she really didn't want to have this discussion and we all continued to her front door.

When we got inside the door, I put my Lincoln Logs in the corner underneath some clothes so that Joie wouldn't ask me anymore questions. I proceeded to plop on the couch and turn on the tube. Joie and Erin whispered something to eachother and announced that they were going to run to the store and would be back in a few minutes.

"Well why didn't you stop while we were out?" I asked.

"Cause I didn't think about it then; Duh!" she snapped back. Why was I not surprised?

About ten minutes after they left, Sam showed up.

I got defensive in my tone. "What? Did I change something else in my future?"

"No, I just thought I should be here right now for two reasons," he said.

"And what would those be?" I said as I kept my defensive tone.

"Well, first, there is about to be a knock at the door and you must not answer it" he firmly replied.

"And why not?" I said, wanting to know.

"Because Michael is coming here to look for Erin and…"

I interrupted "You mean, now, to this apartment?: Well, I've got a few things to say to him"

Sam stopped me mid sentence. "Dawn you can't interfere and if you do talk to him today, it will change a lot of history."

"And how would you know that?" I pressed, "Have you seen something change in the future?" He stood there silent. "What's happened Sam? Is Joie still alive? Is"…

"Dawn, I can't give you any answers, but I am going to take you back to the present this instant, if you open the door or say anything to him. It's not what you want to do, please trust me!" he exclaimed without any room for argument.

Before I could even try and argue, Michael knocked on the door.

My heart was pounding: Sam was watching and I began to sweat. The peephole in the door acted as a lens to capture the image of a murderer for the camera in my eye.

He knocked several times before he twisted the door knob as if to enter.

I'm not sure if I jumped in the coat closet or Sam pulled me in, but I was soon surrounded by darkness and one little strip of light from which to create a video in my mind.

"Erin!!" he yelled angrily.

"Who is he Erin? And where is he at?"

"Erin!!!!"…No answer.

He began checking the bathroom and then the two bedrooms. I seriously hoped he did not have the mentality to think Erin could be hiding in the coat closet. That would only make this situation worse.

As I watched him go through their things, I became even more upset. How could he violate their privacy like that? And why was Sam forbidding me to communicate with him at all? I had questions and I wanted answers.

Michael's pager went off; he grabbed it from his waistline, looked at the number and he was gone as quickly as he illegally had entered.

With the click of the door, I escaped from the darkness and into the light of the front room.

Sam looked at me and told me that he appreciated my trust in him.

"Why did you do that to me?" I rudely asked. "You came here only moments before I had to make an obvious 'life-altering' decision, and you didn't even give me the reason why I had to do it or the agency to make that choice for myself!"

"But…" he interrupted

"Listen Sam, you never gave me a rule book or any kind of silent affirmations that what I have been saying or doing with my sister has been good, bad or indifferent!! Now her killer shows up and you hide me in a closet and expect me to just let him come in here and rummage through their belongings and not even warn him that I'm here?"

"Dawn, these seven days were given to you according to the desires of your heart—You knew you couldn't do anything to change the past, the present or your future. All you are allowed is seven days to say goodbye," he explained.

"What do you mean 'my future'?" I asked curiously.

"Dawn, you need to control two emotions—Love and Hate. These two emotions have altered your future. I only came here tonite, to perhaps turn you towards the path you were already on. Only you can walk it and end where you started this journey" he said calmly.

"What did you mean when you told me that I need to control the two emotions 'Love and Hate'?"

He got up and started to leave. "Love and Hate controls everyone's paths: even Michael's. You need to control these two emotions so that you can understand why you've been given this blessing to be here with Joie"…

He left and the room became empty. My thoughts now turned to my troubled heart.

"Love and Hate", I said out loud.

What a poignant thought. Had my hate changed my future, or was it my love for Joie? I only had 5 more days to figure it all out. But would that be enough time?

I heard Joie and Erin complaining outside their front door about their inadequacies of not ever having an apartment key with them in case of an emergency.

"What emergency?" I asked myself.

"Well you were the last one out Joie, so I know I didn't lock it" Erin said to Joie accusingly.

I looked at the front door and realized that it was locked. Michael had obviously locked it when he left.

I jumped to save the both of them from hypothermia and save myself from having to referee a cat fight with UFO's from Joie's side of the ring. As I opened the door, they both stood there with bags in their hands and the silliest look on their faces.

"So why'd you lock us out?" Joie asked

"Actually I didn't…Michael did" I replied hesitantly.

Erin interrupted "You mean he was here? Tonight? In our apartment?"

I tried to answer her but she kept talking.

"Where were you Dawn? What did he want? What did he say?" she continued.

I reached out to her and took the grocery bag from her, put it on the counter and sat her on the barstool in their kitchen.

"He knocked and I looked through the peephole: And when I saw that it was him, I decided not to answer it; thinking he would just go away. But he turned the door knob several times and I just jumped in the closet and hoped he'd leave. Instead, he came in yelling for you and your new 'boyfriend' and wanted to know where he was at." I said very seriously.

Erin looked nervous. "Did he take anything?"

"No, he just looked through some of your stuff and then his pager/beeper went off and he looked at the number and left the apartment. He must have been the one to lock the door behind him." I finished.

Joie turned from putting up groceries and asked "He didn't use our phone to call anyone did he?"

"I don't think so. He just bolted out of here mumbling something about Erin under his breath." I answered

Erin looked very angry and scared at the same time.

This incident caused me to see Erin in a very fragile way. Michael had really done a number with her. It's not wonder it took Erin so long to leave him and it was an even lesser wonder as to why Joie had become the 'Avenger' of all the wrongs that Michael had done to Erin.

Joie and Erin went into Erin's room to talk and to see if anything was missing. I told them that I would start dinner and give them a holler when it was ready.

I went to the pantry to see what was readily available without having to thaw or marinade anything over five minutes. When I opened the cupboard, Joie's opened bag of spaghetti fell out and started to fly everywhere. Seeing that spaghetti reminded me of the time that Joie and I had gotten home from school and decided to cook a nice meal for our Mom and Pete. They got off work at 5:00 and were usually home by 5:45. So with that in mind, we got started at 3:30 that day, so as to be on time and give them a dinner that they could really sink their teeth into.

Since Pete was Italian, we decided to make spaghetti, salad and garlic bread.

Simple, right?

Joie set the table really nice. I put some water on to boil, and threw the spaghetti in the pot. While that was cooking, we worked together (for maybe the 3rd time in our whole siblingship) on the salad. I chopped the lettuce and tomatoes, while Joie grated (and ate) the cheese. We actually made a great looking salad! We added the necessary ingredients to the Hidden Valley Ranch "Italian" dressing and put it in the fridge to chill.

Next up—the spaghetti sauce.

I fried some hamburger and chopped some onions and added them to some Hunts spaghetti sauce. I put it on low to simmer, and we waited until 5:45 for Mom and Pete to walk through the door.

Just like clock work, they did. Mom was so excited to see the table set and could smell our wonderful Italian dinner.

"What have you guys been doing?" she asked knowingly.

"We thought you'd be tired, so we decided to cook you and Pete an Italian dinner...Spaghetti with salad and garlic bread!" I explained

"How wonderful!" she exclaimed.

We all washed our hands and sat down. Pete said he'd get the spaghetti and the sauce and put it on the table. So there we were: my mom, Joie and me, licking our chops. Pete was at the stove bringing the spaghetti sauce to the table. He asked my mom where the colander was to drain the spaghetti. She told him and we began serving our salad and bread ourselves. Pete stood there silently at the stove.

"What's the matter?" my mom asked.

Joie and I just looked at each other. Pete just stood there with the lid open and asked the three of us to come to the stove.

"Out of sheer curiosity you two, when did you put the spaghetti on to cook?" Pete asked as he held back sarcasm in his small laugh.

I looked at the clock.

"About 3:30 or so…why?" I asked fearing something bad.

My mom shrieked…"You put it on when?"

"What's the matter with that?" Joie chimed in.

As Pete opened the lid to the spaghetti, he said "This is the matter with that!"

And with that he revealed our dinner for that evening…A big fat ball of pasta!

"Where did that come from?" I yelled.

"Well, when you cook spaghetti for OVER two hours, this is what happens!!" Pete laughed.

My mom took one look at it and started laughing too. She tried to offer some help by letting us know that spaghetti only takes 15-20 minutes at the most. Yeah right, now she tells us.

So with our dinner being ruined, I felt defeated and Joie just ate her bread. Keeping our spirits up, Pete grabbed the ball of pasta (now shaped like a small Butterball Turkey) and put it on the table and proceeded to get out the electric carving knife.

My mom could not stop laughing. Pete turned on the knife and started cutting slabs of pasta as big and as round as our plates and giving us each a slice. Then he grabbed the sauce and poured it on our plates.

What a great sport! Instead of making us feel like stupid idiots, he made the best of a bad dinner. And so we had an Italian dinner that night that would not soon be forgotten. Not ever, in fact.

As I finished picking up the spaghetti on Joie's floor, I kept laughing to myself. I had some of the greatest memories in my life because of her. She was always a few bricks short of a load. Yep, my Joie. And now, being here for this last week of her life, meant everything to me.

I just had to figure out how to change it all. And the more I thought about doing that, the more I realized that I was in no way done making such great memories with her. That was that, and I wasn't going to change my mind.

I decided to cook tostadas because we were half mexican and because I knew that Joie loved Elise's version of them.

But I have to admit, no matter how many times I have made them, they don't taste quite the same as if Elise were at the cooking helm. I don't know why that is. Needless to say, I had everything done and ready to go when Joie came out to check my progress.

I informed her that the only thing left to do was to grate the cheese (without her eating it all) and we would be set. Erin asked me if I had made homemade salsa for the tostadas and I told her that this was the one meal that required Pace Picante Medium sauce, and that if she didn't want that for salsa, then to 'get a rope'!.

She laughed and we sat down to eat just a few minutes later.

As we ate, we all talked about so many things. Things that I never imagined that Joie thought so much about. One subject that came up almost instantly was our little brother Brian.

I have always called him Bubba as a nickname. Joie just called him her favorite. That was never a surprise when she said it. And because I was back in 1990, I don't think calling and telling him now would make a difference (because he was only 6 years old at this time) and he didn't comprend Joie's need for bonding. I think that bonding was more intense these days because of her upcoming event (on Sunday) although none of my family knew it at that time.

I knew it, but was bound by the promises I had made to Sam and couldn't change it because it could obviously cost me my eternity in some way. I have always wondered what other people would do if they were given my chance, my situation and wanted the 'obvious' to occur.

As we ate our dinner, Joie offered me her tomatoes.

"Why did you even put them on there if you had no intentions of eating them?" I asked.

"Because that's how I have always made them and then given my unwanted vegetables to you!" she exclaimed.

"But what have you done for the past couple of years when I haven't been around?" I asked puzzled.

"Well I have just gotten them from Taco Bell because they don't put tomatoes on their tostadas, and haven't had to worry about it," she continued, "but now that you're here, I can eat the real thing and give my tomatoes to you.' She finished.

This rationalization reminded me of the times in our life that she had handed me all of her tomatoes from under the table (so as not to get caught) so that she would be allowed to bring her plate to the kitchen and have the rest of the evening to herself. The rule was that you couldn't get up from the table without finishing your dinner (vegetables included).

So with her "Joie" thought process, she always asked me ahead of time (if we were eating tomatoes) if I would eat them for her

And I still believe that to this day, if I hadn't of helped her out, she'd still be sitting at the table trying to 'stomach' them and finish what was on her plate. And as crazy as this sounds, maybe if I hadn't of eaten any of them, then she'd still be at that table in California and this Sunday would have never happened.

I know, I know, my thinking is feudal and very far fetched. But if you can dream the impossible dream, then someday it can happen. My only problem now, is that I have less than five days to change things in a satisfying way so that everyone involved is happy, including Sam.

I still don't know how to change the events of December 3, 1990.

I will admit, that as a person I have tremendously grown from her death, but I want her to stay. I would listen to hours of her off key singing if that's what it meant. I have to think deep and fast. The clock is ticking.

Joie watched me in my pensiveness as I roboticly scraped the dinner dishes into their tiny sink.

"What are you thinking of now?" she asked, not really wanting to know.

"You would never understand; in fact, it would sound completely preposterous" I said.

"Well, however proposterous it may be, it sure has you thinking some DEEP thoughts" she said with a wink.

I finished the dishes and noticed that they were getting ready to "Go Out". I was not prepared to pull another all nighter so I asked if they could stay home and watch T.V. with me. Erin said she told some 'new guy' that she'd meet him at 10:00 and couldn't break her plans because she didn't have his number, so she had to go. I looked at Joie and she actually offered to stay home and watch T.V. with me. Wow, and we didn't even argue about it.

Erin finished getting ready and left soon after. I started to flip through the channels and found the station that played all of the old stuff. "I Love Lucy", "Eight is Enough" and best of all…"Chips"…Remember Ponch and John? As we watched T.V. together, we laughed long and hard. Hearing her laugh again was the most beautiful "music" I had heard in a very long time.

Being in 1990 was somewhat nostalgic for me as well, because I laughed even harder at the commercials from back then. Joie, in her limited 'infinite' humorous side, didn't quite get all the commercials and me, trying to explain some of them to her, well, it just made the product that much more unappealing to her. She spent more time asking "Why would they want to do that?" than actually wanting to buy the product.

That's my sister. Not quite a full deck upstairs, but you gotta love her.

We watched T.V. until about 2am; I finally had to get some shut-eye. As she shut the light off in the front room, I jumped up and hugged her and thanked her for letting me hang out with her tonite. If I could only tell her what I was going through; I think it might explain some of my inexplicable behavior. Not to mention my completely unprovoked and misunderstood body language. I fell asleep trying to find a way to save her.

Day 3

When I woke up on Wednesday morning, I still didn't have a plan. I could feel something inside of my mind, but it was the same kind of feeling you get when you have a word stuck "on the tip of your tongue". I knew it was there, but I just couldn't put my finger on it.

Joie strolled out a little earlier than usual. She reminded me of her photo shoot that afternoon. That meant that I was going to have the privilege of carrying shoes, make-up and whatever else a 'diva' won't carry for herself. So with those tasks at hand and needing to be accomplished today, I started to find my 'Happy Place' that I could escape to later. Everyone needs one of those.

Especially if your sister is a 'diva'.

Erin helped Joie mix and match her outfits accordingly, and they actually asked 'my' opinion on what they looked like. This was strange, because 'my' opinion has always been that plaids can go with stripes. In fact, in high school, Joie would match my outfits for me, so as to help me look a little more 'popular' with a matching outfit. And now, she asked if what she had on looked ok.

Of course, my answer was that it looked great! How would I know the difference anyways? They laughed at me, and said for me to keep my opinion to myself.

We walked out to catch a cab, and the phone started to ring as we were shutting the door. Joie told me to just let the machine get it, because we "can't be late". I knew it was him. The caller. Joie and Erin seemed quite content to come home and listen to his message later. It was really starting to bother me that they took his calls so lightly.

We arrived to the photo shoot with a mere 3 minutes to spare. I had to get my digs in about 'The Caller".

I turned to Joie and said "With these few minutes, we could have answered his call."

Joie paid no attention to my comments, because the photographer walked in. Erin started to primp and spray Joie's hair and touch up her make-up. Joie kept telling Erin "Fix me, Fix me" as she moved her hair from one side to another.

The photographer had obviously shot photos of Joie many times before, because he kept complimenting her on how much her hair had grown, and how beautiful she always looked. Joie admitted that she had had hair extensions put in, and I started to laugh.

"So this is someone else's hair?" I questioned as I picked up a few strands of her 'extensions'.

"That's not funny Dawn, I paid good money to have this done!" she shouted back.

I just laughed. It must cost alot to be a Diva, or like unto it. I do want it to be known, that to be a Diva, one doesn't have to be able to sing. You just have to be able to ask others to do everything else for you, and be able to have hair extensions in your hair at any given time. Yeah, that's how it works. At least that's what I think. Oh, and you also have to have your water from a purified bottling source and not the regular tap. Yeah, that too. And many of us know that Joie was very good at being very demanding.

As I laughed periodically throughout the photo shoot about the different "stupid" mundane poses, I noticed that we had been there for over two hours already. Not that I had anywhere to go, (except to maybe find Michael and detain him so that he would be gone for the rest of the week), but I had to come up with a plan.

All of these photo shoots were diverting my attention to the matter at hand. Saving Joie. In my heart of hearts, I had to do it.

I left the photo room to be alone for a few minutes and gather my thoughts. I actually thought about calling my dad, because he knows alot of people and maybe he could help. But how would I make him believe me? I don't think I would believe me if I were him. I had to have proof. Think Dawn, just think.

I had a great idea. Since I had already been through the 90's, I could simply tell him something before it happened and keep doing that until he was convinced that I was either telling the truth or involved in the Psychic Friends Network. But what woul he believe most out of all the events I could choose?

It wasn't too much longer before Joie and Erin had announced that the shoot was over and my "Diva" assisting services were no longer needed. Humph! Imagine that. I was free to do whatever I wanted to do for the rest of the day.

I wanted to talk to Sam. I wanted to tell him how unfair this whole arrangement is.

How can he send a mortal, who has only a minimal conception of the eternal scheme of things and seriously expect them to adhere to all the rules and not want to change the ending? Especially sending me back with all of my memories and knowledge of Dec. 3? I am prepared to give up or sacrifice whatever it takes to bring her home. I am not leaving here without her. My mind is made up.

I have often times in years past, thought about where she'd be if I could have been the one to go at that particular time in my life. I was prepared even then. Would she be a mom? Would she have gone to college and seriously pursued dance? So many woulda, coulda, shoulda's. And where was Sam for the past 15 years?

He obviously knew her story and for some reason chose me to go through this last week with her. I don't always think with my head. My heart has overridden my head many times because of my inexplicable compassion for anguish such as this. I felt as though all "eyes" were on me to see if I would keep my word. Three days with Joie had convinced me to not uphold my end of the deal.

Surely Sam would listen to reason. He can't be that uncompassionate.

Joie had three bags in her hands and threw one of them at me because she said that she had been asking me for several moments now to help her carry them to the cab outside.

"What on earth are you thinking about Dawn," She asked, finally sounding like she really wanted to know. "And don't tell me it's about some test you have coming up, because you are so lost in you're thoughts, that it seems like you are trying to solve a problem, to which there is no answer and you look so troubled."

I looked at her with such different eyes, longing to tell her what was "really" on my mind.

"Joie, I just want to tell you that I love you and am very thankful that I am here with you at this very moment" I replied as I reached out to hug her.

Erin walked around the corner from getting a pop from the pop machine and saw us hugging and immediately started tormenting me for showing "sisterly love"…

I looked at my watch and realized that it was time to eat. Erin glanced at me and started to laugh.

"Go ahead and make your jokes, but 'fish gotta swim, bird's gotta fly' I need to eat or I'm gonna die!" I sang as best I could in my Barbra Streisand Broadway Album voice.

Joie rolled her eyes and said we could go and eat and do some more Christmas shopping. We got in the cab and were on our way to a strip mall that included Toys R Us.

"What are you getting the rest of the family, Jo?" I asked nosily, even though I had known for 15 years now.

"Well, the one thing I have actually given some thought to, is what to give Brian for Christmas…" she stopped.

"Which is? No wait, let me guess…An electric guitar that has a volume knob that you can break off and drive Dad and Elise crazy with, right?" I said in my dumbest sounding voice.

"How did you know that?" she continued… "I just barely told Erin that last week, and haven't said a word about it to anyone else" she said as she paid the cab driver.

"Oh you told me: you just don't remember telling me" I answered, as I gloated in how much fun I could really have with our conversations.

"What do you mean?" she said with that 'I don't remember our home telephone number' face.

"Joie there are alot of things that I know, but you'd be even more confused if I told you how I really had come to know them".

She just had that blank look/stare on her face and went into Toys R Us to find the biggest and loudest guitar that humor could buy.

Going up and down the aisles of the toys store in search of the "loudest guitar' was Joie's ultimate idea of fun. However, I don't think that the store associates or store's manager saw it quite that way. Erin and I laughed as Joie picked up each guitar and pretended to be an accomplished guitarist and play 'backup' for Van Halen and Whitesnake.

What was even more funny, was that when she tried to play, she had no idea where to put her fingers and especially had no idea to form a chord on the guitar.

Oh, and if you could imagine this site, she was left handed and was trying to hold a concert in Toys R Us as a right handed guitarist. I had to give her an "A" for her efforts.

She had finally found the loudes, most perfect guitar and had also found a toy microphone that came with a cheap amp. You can imagine what happened next.

Joie forgot where she really was and started to give a rock concert to the kids of Toys R Us. She handed a microphone to and to me. Erin decided to live in the moment and sing backup for Joie, who was playing and singing backup for VanHalen/Whitesnake. When in reality was really for Geofrey the Giraffe and his group of friends).

About 30 seconds into her second number, the store manager approached Joie and Erin and I. I knew what he wanted. Joie however, trying to live out her wildest fanatsies (in the music world), quickly reached for her purse. He stopped her right there in the middle of her act on aisle three. Joie, without hesitation, pulled a pen out of her purse and said to the manager "I'll be giving autographs immediately following the show, would you like yours first?".

I could have died. Joie never ceased to make me laugh. What was even more funny, was that she was serious. She had no idea, that he was about to throw us out! I silently hoped that the police weren't already on their way. I assured the manager that she was definitely singing her last number and that we would pay for the guitar and leave without incident.

He smiled and said to hurry up.

Joie finished her stupid song and we went to the checkout to pay for Brian's loud Christmas present. As the manager walked us out to ensure our departure, Joie asked him if he was absolutlely sure, that he didn't want her autograph, "Because I am going to be a star someday" she exclaimed as a parting shot.

"Somehow Ms, I don't doubt it. You have definitely shown your talents here today" he replied as he tried not to laugh under his breath.

Joie started to become flattered and her (already BIG) head started to swell from his facetiousness, and I put my hand over her mouth while Erin shoved her into the cab and told the driver to leave as fast as he could, so that she would have no time to realize what the manager had just said.

All of that because of the love of a little brother and my sister's desire to give him the gift of music and her to desire to give my Dad and Elise the gift of insanity. What a thoughtful person......

I asked Erin and Joie if I could choose the restaurant for dinner that nite...I didn't want the chance of seafood again, so I picked Bob's Big Boy...

Remember those? I do.

Joie and I used to eat there on the weekends when our dad had us. We always got the cheeseburger special that came with that delicious Thousand Island dressing. To this day, no one makes it better.

We ordered and spent a good hour or so just talking and eating...Joie talked about different guys and how she was so picky. I disagreed. I thought both of their tastes in men were not the "Dean Cains" of our day. That's just my opinion. But you'd get a much wittier response of defense from the both of them.

Clearly when the two of them got together, their verbage was not that of School House Rock...I don't even think that Joie knew what a conjunction was or it's function either...And when it came to adjectives, boy they had some words that were never in the songs that I sang...Once could safely say that Joie and Erin rewrote the songs that modified verbs and pronouns without ever knowing it.

We finished dinner and went back to the apartment. Joie had to work so that meant I had two choices, I could go with her and be bored out of my head, or I could stay home in her apartment and devise a plan. As she left, she gave me her work number in case I "changed my mind" and wanted to come down. Only vampires stay up all night. And the last time I checked, I hadn't any fangs in my mouth or any desires to hide from the sunlight...Erin went out with her boyfriend, so that left me alone in my thoughts.

Sam appeared and said hello.

My stomach had a pit in it. I just knew that he wasn't going to let me have her back.

As I said hello to him, he quickly told me that my thoughts were deceiving me. He also told me to not act upon my emotions because they weren't really real and this was just a moment for me to say goodbye.

As I thought about his words, he was right. I had lived all these emotions years earlier…This couldn't happen to me twice could it? He explained that my yearning to bring her back with me would surely destroy what had been planted and grown in her absence the first time. Lives would be altered and the course would not be the true path to take.

I looked up at him with such a heavy glance…"I can't leave her on Sunday, only to die at the hands of another, expecially when I can save her"…

He didn't hesitate to reply "Dawn, try as you may, you won't save her. I will take you back as quickly as you came. Just spend the next few days with her and say all those things you didn't get the chance to say…it's your chance to say goodbye…and I hope when you leave, you will have said things you didn't get to say before"…he continued…" it's not your choice…it's just your chance to do everything necessary to carry you throughout your own destiny without her."

My destiny without her?

I hadn't looked at it like that.

The hardest part of love is trusting in the fact that it circles around again and you are still complete. Whether or not that person is there with you. Sam actually made some sense.

The phone rang and he and I just looked at eachother…I ran to grab it…I really wanted it to be the "Caller"…It was only Joie calling to see if I would come down to the club anyway. I decided to do just that. And with that, Sam was gone.

I sat in the cab thinking about how far I'd come to be at this point. Fifteen years of change and growth without her and knowing that if I brought her back with me, she really wouldn't fit in any of the places of my life that had "grown" into my destiny without her…I had to leave her where I found her.

That alone ripped at my heart and stretched my soul…Sunday was a day not for grieving, but for growing…

As the cab stopped at Memories, I jumped out, paid him and went inside to what would probably be another all nighter…I shouldn't complain, except for the fact that I was always the "monkey" on display when Joie described me as her "Goody Two Shoes" sister…People in the club acted like I had a rare disease. Not drinking or smoking was a new concept to them. Well, it wasn't to me…

I just drank alot of soda…The Manager who comped my "drinks", just laughed everytime I asked for a refill…it was there, at Memories, that I realized just how great Dr. Pepper tastes. Wouldn't you like to be a Pepper too?

Joie came and sat with me on her breaks. It was that night that I started to memorize her face again. Her laughter and her bad breath. Joie had the worst breath ever.

No matter how many times she brushed her teeth, it just stayed BAD…I remember all the times that we'd go out to eat with my Dad and Elise and they would always make her eat parsley. That is supposed to help bad breath evidently. Well, we'd always end up giving her the parsley off our plates. Just watching her gag as she tried to eat it, made my breath start to stink. Yuck…Poor little off-key Rock Star, with the poor little bad breath syndrome. Man was that a combo…And she was blessed with both…

In the background of all the activities going on, I heard a commotion by the door. I looked up to see Erin fighting with Michael.

I jumped out of the booth and ran towards him. He had her by the arm and wouldn't let her go until she "talked" with him. I pushed him as hard as I could and as he let go of her, he came towards me. The manager ran in between us and told Michael to leave because he had called the cops. Michael refused. My heart was pounding with fear, but I had to lash out at him…He was bigger than me, but that didn't matter to me…My only thoughts were of his selfish acts to come. I was relentless in my pursuit for vengence towards him. And out of nowhere I could hear those words again. "Love and Hate are the two emotions I needed to control"…The sirens got louder and the music came to a lull…The cops were there and I still hadn't had my chance with Michael…

Day 4

Michael wanted the officers to take "his statement"…Michael's plea fell on deaf ears…He just didn't get it…The first sign of obsession in my opinion, would be how he couldn't hear anyone but Erin. The police were trying to talk to him, but he was locked on Erins every move and hung on her every word. The cops had seen and heard enough.

Michael was arrested and taken away in the squad car at about 1:45 am. I was beat and ready to turn into a pumpkin. Joie said she had about two more shows and then we could go. No more soda for me. I was floating now…

As the music played, I remembered each song from when I was in college that first time, with all my friends.

Erin came and sat down with me and I asked her how she was doing. She explained that Michael had been harassing her for some time since she'd left him.

"He just won't let go of me"…she said slowly…"I have moved on and he doesn't want to let go"…

"Maybe a night in the slammer will cause him to realize that he is not in control anymore…" I said almost prophetically…as well as not being able to tell Erin that Michael would spend the rest of his life in the slammer.

"He scares me…" she mumbled above the loud music…"I never know where he's going to strike out at me next"…

"Why don't you get a restraining order against him?" I asked.

"It wouldn't do any good…he'd still come around and harrass me"…she said sounding defeated already.

I looked at my watch, and finally just took it off and put in my pocket, so that the water might boil in my watchpot…And maybe, just maybe, sunlight would be here sooner than Christmas.

I was starting to get really sleepy…I just wanted to absorb every second of Joie's laughter and beauty. Every second…

Joie came and sat with me in between her routines and tried to comfort Erin. Joie wasn't the most brilliant kid on the block, but she loved Erin. She wanted to be a source of help for her. I could only sit there and feel my heart break as Joie tried to cheer Erin up with thoughts of how they would be roommates for-ever and conquer the world. I could sure use that off key rock band right about now, singing me an off key song to take my mind off of the inevitable…

It was 5:30 AM when we got home. That couch looked so comfortable. Actually, I could have slept outside in the snow, and still felt that good…

Erin volunteered to take the couch and offered the bed to me, so that I could have a "slumber" party with Joie…

It started out ok, but then before too long, Joie and I were in a debate about Rick Springfield and he'd done "Everything for her"…At least that was her side of the story…She jumped up and flipped on the light and started to swim through her piles and piles of clothes on the ground.

"What are you doing?" I asked almost knowingly…

"Looking for…" she dove to the floor…"THIS!!"…She exclaimed as she waved a cassette tape of Rick Springfield's 'Working Class Dog'…

I just laughed…Laughed at the sea of clothes she swam through just to find it, and laughed at how funny it was to see a "cassette"…I had an amazing thought about that moment, and how much more fun Joie would have had if she could have seen the Cd's coming out…Knowing her, she would have chuckled it at me like a frisbee…

We put the music on and started to laugh…

Jesse was a friend…yeah…sure he was…It all came back…Note by note, line by line…

And to make it more enjoyable, Joie sang it with such conviction in each note that was at least 2 half steps below the orginal key…Poor little off key singer, still can't find her off key rock band…Not even Rick would help her out…

By about 6:45AM (that was the last time I looked at the clock) I was zonked…I fell asleep from being tired, yet started to dream myself wide awake, so as to find a way to save her…

(In my dream it was easy…Leave her apt, come back and save her…That was simple…Well, in my dream, I made sure that Sam wasn't a leading character. In my dream, they were my rules and my choices. Nothing but happiness for those choices. Everytime I had a question, there was an answer…This is what I am talking about…It all fit together.)

At about 10:30 am, I got up because I didn't want to sleep my days away with Joie that I needed to share with her…She got mad, but I nudged her to wake up as well…

Joie was never a morning person…She was a beast…You could never get her out of bed before noon…School work suffered because of her lack of desire…

Oddly enough, her circle of friends had the same sleeping principles as she. So needless to say, her social life didn't lack for anything…

I thought it might be fun to clean up her disaster zoned apartment…Seeing her room reminded me of the time that we lived with our mom in Maryland

and shared the attic together. Our step-father Pete had asked us (Joie) several times to clean up the attic or else he'd do it himself…

Well, Joie never heard his bidding (or so she says)…So one day as we got off the bus, we were walking towards my mom's house. And I saw the most amazing thing…

There in the distance, was Pete with a snow shovel and shoveling out every last piece of Joie's clothing out the third story window…I started to point and laugh…She started running and screaming obscenities at him…I couldn't stop laughing. I thought it was classic…As Joie ran, for what seemed like the fastest time in the 100 meter dash, I kept watching the shower of clothes floating down to the earth…Joie was scrambling to pick them up, run them back upstairs just to get the next shovel he had shoveled out…Well, this went on for at least ten minutes…Then I stopped laughing…

He was shoveling my stuff too…That was not funny…Joie was the slob…Not me…I grabbed my clothes and wasn't dumb enough to put it back in the room just so he could shovel it out to the ground again. Joie just kept repeating her cycle…Kind of like the instructions on a shampoo bottle…Lather, Rinse, Repeat. Where does it ever end?

Needless to say, Joie missed her favorite afternoon shows that day…What a flashback…Maybe Pete did it because he was finally getting back at us for breaking his chess set years earlier…Too much, I tell ya…

Her apartment sure needed a face lift now…But where would I begin? I don't think that Joie had vaccumed in her entire stay in that apartment…You get the picture…It needed a serious Extreme Makeover…

I got out the Hefty bags and started to seperate the clothes…What a mess…Joie started to complain that she knew where "everything" was at, and that I was messing up their system of logic…Right…I don't think that even a blood hound could have found one solid scent…It all meshed together…That was Joie…Everything in disarray and she liked it like that…

Why?

I don't think anyone could ever know…

The phone rang at about 11 am…It was him…

"The Caller" was consistent. I ran to the phone.

"Hello?" I said, thinking he'd actually make himself known.

No response…Just a sigh and a hint of disappointment in his breathing…

"Look, I don't know who you are, but you picked the wrong girl to call"…I said with a serious tone.

Click…

He was gone…

Joie and Erin bragged that they could have gotten a better response if either one of them had answered. That's just what I needed to hear…

"Do you guys provoke him?" I asked in a dumb way.

"No we just tease him"…Erin explained.

"That's not safe, you know that?" I replied.

Joie walked into the kitchen and poured herself a bowl of cereal.

I quickly mentioned as she was pouring the milk on her cereal that the milk was outdated…And you should have seen the look on her face.

"Will you pleeeaazzee go to the store and buy some more?"…she begged.

"No way…I have to clean up this joint. You get off your keister and go get it yourself"…I said sarcastically.

"But then I'll have to shower and get ready"…she said as she whined.

"Just throw a cap on your head...it's only a few blocks to the corner store"...

"Are you serious?" she snapped..."I don't go outside without my clothes and make-up on"...

"Well then I guess you're going to starve...cause I am not going to get you some milk"...I continued..."Maybe next time you won't feed me seafood and I'll be inclined to run some errands for you in return...see how that works?" I quipped.

"Fine, but the next time you want me to match your clothes, DON'T ASK...because I don't care if you put plaid with stripes...I'll just let you look like a dork" she yelled...

Erin jumped in the middle of what was about to become a wrestling match...

"Ok...ok...I'll go and get some milk and you two can hug and love each other."...she said...

I thought it would be classic at that moment to do just that...Just to yank Joie's chain...

As I leaned forward to hug her, she punched me in the stomach and ran for her life...yeah...I was going clean her clock and she knew it.

As I chased her she screamed and laughed...I could never keep up with her...If I got in her space, she scratched me...

I jumped on her to tackle her...She went down like a bowling pin...I grabbed her arms and sat on her legs and started to tickle her...Then I started to pinch her...She was kicking and screaming and then she did the unthinkable...

She spit on me...

Man...that really set me on fire...

So I spit on her in return.

Erin was laughing as she took off for the store to get the culprit that had started this all...Some fresh milk.

As I was trying to keep Joie under control, the phone rang again. She punched me and jumped up.

"Hello?" She said.

As she started talking, I could tell it wasn't 'the caller'. I continued to pick up a around the house. You wouldn't believe the things that these two dropped on the floor. I was expecting to find bugs nesting amongst the expensive clothing that neither of them took care of. To my surprise, I found nothing. But when I had finished separating all the laundry, I knew that it would take Erin and Joie and their entire circle of friends to help them out at the laundromat. Not too mention, they would have to rob a bank to be able to afford all those loads of laundry.

Joie came in and announced that a photographer needed her to come in for a few minutes for some shots for his magazine. Apparently, the first model he hired, wasn't as reliable and never showed. So he called Joie and before I knew it, we were packing up to shoot another roll of the diva. Yep, that meant I was back on duty as the official grunt.

Erin arrived back at the apartment with some fresh milk as Joie was getting out of the shower. She asked Joie if she needed her to come along and Joie told her no. She said it wouldn't take long and that we'd be back in about an hour.

"Yeah, right" I said as I rolled my eyes at Joie.

"He only wants two poses and one outfit...How can that take longer than an hour?" she asked, like I hadn't been to any other photo shoots this week.

We took a cab there and the photographer was actually very organized. He spent his time waiting on Joie, rather than her waiting on him. I was impressed with him because he only photographed her from the shoulders up. He kept telling us that he wanted to capture her beauty, not her body. Not bad.

As we waited for a couple of minutes for him to change his roll of film, Joie asked me to get her some water from a bottle.

"Why can't you just drink it from the water fountain?" I joked

"Because the water splashes on my face and ruins my makeup!" she said as if I should know stuff like that.

I wandered out into the hall and found a water dispenser. Of course I had to buy it. She didn't offer to give me a buck!

I came back in with the water and she guzzled it down.

"I thought divas drank water with a little more class than that" I said with a wink.

"Sometimes we take our 'crowns' off and just slam it!" she retorted...

As we neared the end of the photo shoot, a very strange thought occurred to me. This photographer would be the last man to photograph Joie. And as he snapped the last shot, I realized that that would be the very last picture taken of Joie on this earth.

He thanked her for showing up on such short notice and told her that he'd call her next week for the proof review. We, meaning I, gathered all her things and carried them out to the waiting cab. We got in and she told him to head home.

As we arrived, the UPS guy was leaving in his truck. Joie jumped out and tried to flag him down. Let it be known, that she is not bionic.

She walked into her apartment thinking she'd have to call UPS and have them re-deliver, until Erin yelled from the bathroom that she had signed for it.

"You did? Well where is it?" she asked.

"It's on your bed. I didn't know if you wanted Dawn to see it now or later!" she answered back.

Joie ran to her room and told me to stay out. She shut the door and within moments I could hear her unwrapping the only Christmas present that had more value than anything I'd ever received: An Elvis Collector's Plate.

As she came out empty handed, I assumed that the plate would now be lost in the abyss. But much to my surprise, she announced that my gift had arrived in perfect condition and that as soon as she had it wrapped, she'd give it to me to open.

That made a lot of sense. She was notorious for things like that.

Erin yelled for Joie to come in the bathroom. Joie walked in and shut the door.

Within a few seconds, she was grabbing me and we were headed to the store. It only took a few minutes by cab and I still had no idea what we were getting.

"What are we getting now" I asked.

"Erin needs some 'stuff' from the store" she said trying not to give it away.

"What kind of 'stuff'?" I asked.

We walked in to the grocery store and Joie made a beeline to the 'aisle'. I had a funny flashback as she stood there and searched for Erin's 'stuff'.

Years back when Joie was still living at home with our dad and Elise, she had gone with him to the grocery store. As they entered the store, Joie headed for the magazines, to check out all the new fashions and such.

My dad only needed a couple of things and told Joie he'd be right back. So being the prankster that he is, he did come right back. Joie was reading the magazines when these two cute boys came and picked up some motorcycle magazines and began reading.

Joie, being the little flirt, started trying to get there attention.

Well, my dad wouldn't have any of that. He called to Joie from the end of the aisle.

"Joie?" he said

"Yeah dad?" she said trying to turn towards the two boys.

"The tampons on are on aisle seven!" he yelled as he walked off.

You should have seen her. She was livid. She threw that magazine down and hid her face and fled to another part of the store. All the while, screaming at our dad. He was laughing so hard. It was a classic moment. One that ranks in his top ten things to always remember.

Now, here, at the store, Joie is first to mention that she'll gouge my eyes out if I make any comments like unto those from years ago. I start to chuckle to myself.

"Of course, your highness, I wouldn't dream of humiliating you on this aisle!" I shot back.

She plucked the box of 'stuff' off the shelf and told me to get the lead out so we could get home without incident.

My guess is, that every time she has to buy those things, she can always hear dad saying "The tampons are on aisle seven!"

We get back to the apartment and Erin was happy because Joie saved the day. The phone rang almost as soon as we got back and it was Michael leaving a message from jail.

"Don't answer it Jo-let me him finish his stupid message" I suggested.

Joie hit the 'delete' button as soon as he was finished. She seemed unphased by his obsession with Erin. But Erin's demeanor seemed 'cautious' whenever his name floated through the air.

It started to get a bit cold in the apartment and I asked Joie to turn the heat up. She just looked at me and told me that since I wasn't paying the heating bills,

I'd have to bundle up. And with that, she tossed me a big white afghan that our Nana had made for her.

Sam showed up and told me how angry Michael really was.

"And what am I supposed to with that?" I asked

"He is consumed with getting her back" he replied.

"Well, if I can't interact with him and at least tell him to stay away-then what good does it do me to care about what you're saying" I questioned.

"I told you that he would have trouble with 'Love and Hate' and I am wanting you to overcome your emotions because like his are doing, yours will deceive you as well" he explained.

I sat and thought about what he was telling me. Somehow I knew that he knew more than he let on. It wasn't so much that he was an angel giving me this opportunity, it was like he was on my level of sorts. I just couldn't figure out his cryptic message.

"By the way Dawn, that photo shoot today was a bonus: you got to witness the last photo of Joie to ever be taken." he said.

"What do you mean?" I said, thinking that that was how it had happened before.

"She didn't fill in the first time for that girl" he continued "Events from the club last night changed that outcome and caused the photographer to have to utilize Joie at the last moment today...It wasn't part of the 'weeks events'" he finsished.

I just looked at him and tried to completely understand the magnitude of what he had just told me. I had been given something extra. I didn't realize it until he pointed it out for me.

As he left, he mentioned to me that if at all possible, to try and talk to Erin about getting the police involved upon his release from jail...

So now he was giving me evasive clues to perhaps change the outcome? It didn't seem like his style. Let alone, Erin's to actually utilize the protection of the police.

Joie asked if I wanted chinese food for dinner.

"It's better than seafood, so why not?" I joked.

"Well if it's free, why do you care anyway?" she said sarcasticly…

That was a true statement. And if she was buying, then I am eating.

I looked at the clock. It was a little after eight. No wonder I was hungry.

Since we were eating dinner at home and it was so late already, I told Joie that if we didn't go out, then I'd make cookies. Upon hearing that, she said ok. Erin chimed in with "At least you have fresh milk to drink with the cookies!"…

We all laughed.

While waiting for the take out to arrive, Joie jumped in the shower. I swear that girl showered like five times a day.

She must of only been in there for just a couple of minutes, when I heard a thud…Erin and I jumped up and knocked on the door. Joie yelled back that she was ok, but had just fallen like she was on a slip-n-slide. Now that was funny. It brought to mind one of the most notorious things we did as youngsters.

Erin and I sat on the couch and proceeded to tell her the most hilarious memory to date.

Years back when Joie and I were still toddlers, our Nana and Tata took us every summer on vacation to Mexico or somewhere in the mountains. Our cousin Lisa (who is the same age as me) accompanied us on those journeys. The three of us were little terrors. Just ask Nana. Our Tata would always complain to

Nana and say: "God bless it, just once I'd like to go on vacation without these grandkids!"...Our Nana would put him in his place for comments like that.

This one summer they took all three of us to Mexico. But this was the year that we had finally convinced Nana that we were big girls and could go to the showers alone and bathe ourselves. We just felt cramped in the trailer shower. I mean have you ever showered in those? They're teeny.

So Nana packed our little bags full of soap and shampoo, etc. And we were off...It was a little hike for two five year olds and one three year old. But we did it. Lisa and I were in charge of Joie. That was Nana's first mistake. Never give a five year old Aries the power over a three year old. It spells D-I-S-A-S-T-E-R...

We got to the little shower room and noticed the cleaning lady just finishing up the floors. We waited for a couple of minutes until she was done. She left and we unpacked our things.

About an hour had passed and Nana hadn't seen hide nor hair of any of us. So she started to wonder. Then it happened. There was a knock on the trailer door. Nana opened it up, only to find the cleaning lady yelling at her in spanish...

Nana knew exactly what she was saying. She grabbed her keys and followed her to the little shower in the woods.

All good things come to an end.

As the bathroom door opened, we didn't notice our Nana just standing and watching. We were having way too much fun.

I had gotten this brilliant idea to turn all the faucets on and plug the sinks so that the water ran over onto the floor. As the floor became completely immersed, I told Lisa to grab her shampoo bottle and I grabbed mine, and we dumped it all over the floor.

I had just designed the worlds largest slip-n-slide!!

We all took our clothes off and started sliding from one end of the bathroom to the other on our bare butts!! The floor was slick and fast!! We were on top of our game.

Until the room roared with thunder.

Nana was screaming and yelling at us in spanish and we jumped up and started to run! She was chasing us and trying to whip our bare butts. We ran. Joie looked like the only innocent one.

Of course Nana thought I was the ring leader. So we bolted out of there stark naked. Running for our lives, back to the trailer. No towels or clothes. Just soapy naked bodies!

After running for what seemed like ten miles, Nana caught up to Lisa and I. She started whipping us...Yeah, whipping us...She said we would never be allowed to go to the showers alone again...Just because we were having a little bit of fun.

Erin was laughing so loud at this point, that Joie poked her head out of the shower and asked what was so funny.

"Dawn was just telling me about your adventures in Mexico and the giant sli-n-slide" she laughed

"Oh, that story...Yeah, every word of it is true!" she said shutting the bathroom door.

Dinner arrived rather quickly and I just started eating. Joie and Erin saw great humor in their fortunes.

I found mine rather amusing because it said: "A big adventure awaits you."

Kind of ironic, I think.

We finished dinner and I made the cookies. I am surprised we had any, seeing as how Joie kept eating the cookie dough. And wouldn't you know she hardly ate any of the cooked ones because of all the dough she had consumed.

Erin was flipping through the channels on tv and came across "Annie"…That was our absolute favorite.

Joie and I recited every single line of that movie. Erin had to keep telling us to shut up. We didn't though. Every time a good part would come on, we'd say the same thing "Oh, this is cool, watch this!"…

I think Erin wanted to pelt us both. I am going to assume that she wanted to smack Joie more than I because of her singing during the musical numbers. Poor little rock star-never gonna find her off key rock band!

We finished the evening with a dance routine and by singing "I Don't Need Anything But You"…

Erin was in stitches from Joie's impersonation of Miss Hannigan. I thought our rendition of "Sign" was classic. But then again, you should have seen her drunk routine to "Little Girls"…

Now must people would pay top dollar for that Broadway musical, but Erin got it for free. Somehow, the look on her face didn't seem like she appreciated the compd. performance of "Annie"…

I have this feeling, that she was wishing she'd of never stumbled upon that channel. Joie and I were quite glad. The only sad thing about it, was that when it was over, it was getting late.

I was actually tired. I didn't want to sleep, because every minute counted with Joie and I. But my lack of sleep was giving me a headache and I need to rest for what lay ahead.

Erin called Greg and he came and picked her up. Joie and I cleaned up the kitchen and put the cookies in some 'unopened' tupperware and called it a night.

I gave her a hug and told her what a great day I'd had. She smiled and said "Me too Dawn…Me too".

Day 5

Two days left. I felt the sweat on my brow amidst the cold December air on my only morning walk. Sam was nowhere to be found. Michael had been released from jail and Erin had a different look in her eyes now. To save Joie would take a miracle.

Still though, this had been an incredible week. We had talked about many things and as such have even included a most prophetic look at her upcoming death on Sunday. To date, I hadn't changed a single occurrence that would unfold on Sunday. But why? Perhaps subconsciously, you just know not to mess with an angel.

Sam must not have ever lost someone.

As I realized the air was actually cold and that I was no longer sweating, but freezing, the sun came up. I started walking back to Joie's apartment. Sam was up just ahead by the corner store.

"What's wrong now" I asked

"Nothing" he said, "Just wondering why you're out here."

"Actually? I was thinking of a way to break all the rules and bring her home with me." I said facetiously.

"You aren't serious" he replied in the same tone.

"I was, and of course, I ran through all the reasons why and then it occurred to me…" I stopped.

""What did?" he asked

"It occurred to me that you can't ask me to not stop her death—you are only an angel and have never grieved like me" I said with a slight pause.

"What does that mean?" he questioned.

"Have you ever lost someone you love? I mean you guys are already in heaven, so you don't exist here—so to speak."

"Dawn, there are rules given to everyone, no matter where they are from…What you don't know is the beginning to the end or vice versa. Every choice comes with a consequence—good or bad."

I interrupted "But wouldn't you want to save someone if it meant bringing happiness to so many other's lives?"

He continued, "It doesn't matter what I would want in your situation, and I don't know your grief, it's true, because that grief is yours and yours alone—So I couldn't possibly understand what your life or her life means to you…Still, that does not give you the latitude in changing the events that have already happened or changing the future you already know just because you can't control those two emotions: Love and Hate."

He said it again. Those words. They must mean something or he wouldn't use them so emphatically.

"Love and hate?" I asked.

"I told you that you need to control those emotions. They are very powerful and have been a mode of destruction that cannot be reversed." He said as if he'd seen it himself.

"I know Michael's hate is what killed Joie and we found her too late and nothing could be reversed. I realize that. I understand what you're saying."

"It's more than that" he responded.

"You don't know the mortal pain or grief that comes from losing Joie" I argued.

"Look, we've been over this and you know the rules. Just spend your last 48 hours with her and you're going back. End of story"

And with that, he was gone...

It would be the end of my story. Not hers. I had to save her. No matter the cost.

I was starting to cook breakfast and noticed the laundry in a pile on the floor that Joie had neglected. As I began to fold her clothes, I put them to my face to smell them. I had forgotten so many things. Her laugh, her wit and even her capacity to reason. She had been gone so long, that the littler things had finally slipped my memory.

As I got closer to the bottom of the pile, I noticed her Christmas presents in the corner ready to mail home. I picked up the box for me. She had somehow found the time to write the now infamous last letter to me. On my Elvis Plate Box she had written:

Dawn,

> Please take care of this. It was not cheap and it's a collector's item. You break this and you die. Take care, it's been a banner year.

Your Sis,

Jo

Go figure. She had had a vision beyond her own comprehension. It really had been a banner year that year. More importantly, it had been a banner week.

I left the packages exactly as I had found them. I left some unfolded clothes mostly covering them so she wouldn't know that I had read the box early.

In my soul I was crying. On the outside I was so angry. Why couldn't I warn her? Even if could get her to leave town for the day. Anything. Just then, the fire alarm went off from the smoky bacon. As I jumped up to fan the air around the alarm, Joie walked into the kitchen.

"Bacon?" she said with one eye open "I love bacon!"

"Well don't eat but one piece, because it will be ready in about 15-20 minutes," I said.

In the middle of breakfast she must have read my mind, because she stopped me and asked what I was so pensive about.

"Pensive? Did you say pensive?" I asked, not knowing she even knew that word.

"I know I appear dumb, but I'm really not" she countered.

I just looked at her.

"Dawn, you've been thinking about something since we sat down…I just want to know what it is" she said.

"I don't know" I said "I guess I was just thinking about leaving on Sunday and how we have so much left to do" I admitted.

"Well I don't know why you're worried, you can always come back and see me" she exclaimed glamourously.

"I suppose" I said with a lump in my throat.

She was right though. I could do just that.

❦   ❦   ❦

Erin had to do some more Christmas shopping, so Joie elected to spend the day with me. I got in the shower and got ready for the day: still hearing Sam's words of "Love and Hate" all the while.

When I was finished in the bathroom, I found Joie watching QVC. That instantly reminded me of the time when we were in high school and our mom had coerced Joie in to calling the network channel and doing something that only Joie could do…One of Joie's hidden talents is that she does a mean impersonation of Bobcat Goldthwait. Yeah, the screaming comic…

Joie had seen a fur coat she liked and decided to call in and go "on-air"…Well the ladies on the show had no idea what was about to hit them. Joie did her best "Bobcat" voice and asked if they had layaway on that coat…But she didn't ask like you or I might, she used her high pitched screechy voice and exclaimed "Uh, yeah, uh, yeah, do you have, have, laya-lay-uh…Way?"…Our mom peed her pants over that one.

"Joie—I need some advice"

"Well Dawn, my first words of wisdom to you are always remember that jeans go with everything." she said as she threw her head back in laughter.

"Ha. Ha. Very funny—I'm being serious" I said as I smacked her head.

She immediately wiped the smile from her face and gave me a serious poker face.

"How's this look?" she asked with a grin.

I tried not to crack a smile, but it was too late. She could be pretty funny. I gave in and busted up. We laughed for several seconds.

"Jo~ What do you think it means to control 'love and hate' or the consequences are irreversible"

She just looked at me with a blank stare.

"What kind of question is that?" she said with that "deer in the headlights" look.

"Just wondered if you knew what that meant" I asked, now knowing she didn't care one way or another.

I got up and shut the television off and turned on the radio. It was then that Sam entered the room. I knew that Joie couldn't see or hear him, so I just let the music play while he spoke.

"You can't ask her things like that" he said.

Joie got up and changed the station to some eighties station, then started dancing and singing.

"You can't give her clues or ask her about things that I have shared with you—she's not on that level. Your time is nearly done and you can't change anything. End of story".

Sam kept talking, but I just didn't want to hear it so I tuned him out.

Joie started talking to me at the same time. The phone rang—I couldn't wait to talk to "the caller". We both ran for the phone, but she beat me…Running those short distance races always takes me back to our toilet fights. She had to always have the same toilet as me, just to yank my chain.

"Hello?" Joie said. "Hi Mom…No—that's just the radio…He called yesterday…Oh, she's out Christmas shopping…Oh…yeah, that loser got out of jail…Probably told some lie, I don't know. He just doesn't get it…No, Eric has Holly…Sunday or Monday I think…ok…Love you more…" Click.

Sam was still babbling and then the moment changed. The radio station put on "Somewhere Out There". Joie started singing it at the top of her lungs while dancing in some other place. Poor little rock star, can't find her off key rock band.

"Somewhere Out There" was a song our mom had loved a lot and always told us to listen to it whenever it came on the radio. She said it was because the three of us always lived apart from one another and it made her feel like we were still under the same moon as the lyrics made mention of.

What was even more emotional for me, was that I sang that song at Joie's funeral. It was probably the most difficult song I have ever struggled to sing in tune.

Crying and singing are very hard to do at the same time. Grief comes in and the next thing you know, you're singing off key. But the song hit a chord in my soul that I hadn't recalled since that day long ago. The pain was more than I remembered. Funny how time does heal your wounds and you do start to recover and mend.

I sat there and watched her dance to it. This would be a much better memory for me to have of this song now. At least I could see her dancing to it instead of remembering how she looked laying there in her casket. Don't get me wrong, she looked beautiful, but it's the only memory I have to the song whenever I hear it. This was definitely a much more beautiful way to "hear" the song.

Sam left. I guess he was frustrated, just like me. I just can't figure it out. Sam has used that metaphor several times now. Love is the opposite of hate. You can't do both. It's like the scripture: "No man can serve two masters."

But what does that mean? Don't hate Michael? Love Michael? Love Joie? Hate Sunday? I don't know. I needed more information from Sam. No chance of that happening any time soon.

I asked Joie if she wanted to go roller-skating. Surprisingly, she said yes without even a fight. As we rode in the cab to the rink, I remembered all the times that we went skating as kids in California. My first pair of skates were the one that strapped on my tennis shoes. Remember those? Plastic sliding "one-size-fits-all" skates from Fisher Price…I had them cracked and broken in no time…Actually, my feet were just too darn big for my body. Joie's skates never broke. Even at an early age, she had such a sense of grace. Me? I don't think Grace lived anywhere on the street. Either that, or she just didn't like me.

We paid the cab driver and went into the rink and found those old skates with smelly souls…Joie was the first on the floor and of course, the first to fall. She was ok the first few times she fell because of her perfect bubble butt padding.

Before too long we were flinging each other around the corners at record speeds. I was made for the speed. Joie was made for the walls. She almost looked like the perfect picture frame every time she smacked into one. I had to laugh at her, because for having such grace when she danced, she realized that age and gravity were now playing a big role in her roller skating abilities.

We did the "Hokey Pokey" and turned ourselves around because that's what it's all about…Right? You can only do the Hokey Pokey if you know your left hand from your right. Well, that leaves Joie still turning herself around, because that's what she's all about.

As the hours wore on, we got a tad hungry and hit the snack bar. You have to keep your skates on, you know? I was ok with the nachos and the pretzels, but Joie couldn't handle the drink carrying and skating to our booth without becoming a little wobbly.

My feet were sore. I always get that way when I have to skate in circles in one direction. It's always nice when they call "Reverse Skate"…I love going the other way. Much like I should do on Sunday. "Reverse Skate" with Joie out of town.

The session was done and we were dog tired. We caught a cab and picked up a video on the way home. Video? I haven't used a VCR tape in ages. I banished the very thought of every trying to explain the concept of a DVD to Joie.

Joie roamed up and down each aisle until she had found the perfect movie:

"Girls Just Wanna Have Fun". If you've ever seen the movie then you know exactly what I am talking about. A young Sarah Jessica Parker and Helen Hunt show us how to become regulars on D-TV. The movie is a classic.

When we finally got home with the video of the year for the past 10 years, we ate like pigs and watched it two times before Joie fell asleep.

As I sat on the couch beside her I just memorized her face all over again. It was rare to see her in the "downtime" mode, so I let her sleep.

I cleaned up a bit, turned off the television, turned the radio off (she'd had it on low all day) and threw a blanket her on and went to bed.

It was a very rough night. I knew when I woke up the next morning that I'd only have a day and a half left. I started calling out for Sam, but he never showed.

I don't know exactly what time it was, but it was not bath time. Joie had gotten up and dumped water on my head while I had slept. I woke up and heard her yelling at me to either scoot over and share the bed or to get out and find the couch.

As I lay there with a wet head—her antics reminded me of the time when we were three and five and were spending the weekend with our dad. Our dad has a tremendous snoring problem, even to this day.

Well, our dad kept snoring most the night and Joie being a young, loving daughter thought he might be thirsty. I would have had to agree. I mean after all, he would open his mouth when he snored like he hadn't any hydration in days. So Joie got out of bed, got a glass of water and came to his side and just waited. And wouldn't you know it, he was thirsty. So much in fact, that the next time he opened his mouth to snore, Joie dumped the entire glass of water in his mouth!

You should have seen him choke! He woke up gasping for air and we took off. We were running the fifty yard dash in world record time. We ended up under a bed, just out of his reach until morning. To this day, he is still thirsty. Guess that one glass wasn't enough.

Joie and I laughed over that story. She finds herself mildy amusing. I think that she could bring down the house with laughter.

It was very early in the morning and I needed a few good hours of sleep to devise a plan that would not be the "End of Story" as Sam would say.

Day 6

Thank goodness Erin crawled in at noon, or we'd of kept on sleeping. I snagged the shower first because Joie and Erin seemed to have a love affair with the hot water every time they went before me: which left me nothing but a cold shower and a short lived relationship.

When I got out of the shower, the pizza guy was delivering their home cooked lunch.

"Pizza?" I complained.

"What's wrong with pizza?" Erin asked.

"Nothing, if you like choking on cheese!" I said in my defense.

"She's weird Erin, don't even pay attention to her" Joie said as she tossed the pizza boxes on the table.

We ate lunch and talked about Christmas. That was a very significant thing for me. Because when Joie had died, it ruined not only that first Christmas, but all the years after that. It's something my mother never recovered from. We talked about Brian's guitar and how funny it would be when he played it and drove my dad and Elise crazy. Joie and her plans. You had to love the fact that in the end, it was ironic for all those gifts to take on their destiny in a way.

By about three in the afternoon, the girls were ready to go again. Joie had to work that night and I really didn't want to do the club thing again. In reality, it would be my last night with her before I had to leave for good tomorrow.

It's hard to keep your thoughts in check. There is a mantle that comes with this gift of saying goodbye. Had anyone else ever been given the chance and just blew it? Why was my soul ok with changing my eternity as well as hers?

I had to swallow harder so that the pit in my throat didn't come up.

The phone rang again and this time it was him. Erin kept him talking (or breathing) for at least three or four minutes.

"Why do you guys antagonize him?" I asked, scolding her.

"We don't, we just bug him until he hangs up" she countered.

Joie jumped in~ "He's no harm, and we think we know who it is"

I cut her off. "Who?"

"Some regular at the club" Erin said.

"And you think this because…?"

"One of the girls heard him bragging one night at the club about how he love to call single women and scare them" Joie explained.

"But we don't scare easily" Erin joked.

"Dawn, I need to talk to you" Sam said out of nowhere.

"What?" I asked.

"But we don't scare easily" Erin repeated.

"No I heard that Erin…never mind" I said.

"Dawn in a few minutes there will be a knock at the door and it will be Michael…You can't interfere or say anything to him" he warned.

Without hesitation, there it was. The knock. My blood began to boil and my emotions changed to anger almost instantly.

"Don't open it Joie!" I shouted.

Joie looked through the peephole.

"It's Michael" she whispered to Erin.

"What is he doing here?" I asked with an edge to my voice.

"I don't' know, but someone needs to get rid of him!!" Erin pleaded.

Joie opened the door only slightly, due to the only form of security on the door…a rinky dink chain.

"What do you want?" Joie asked rudely.

"None of your business!" he yelled…"Where's Erin?"

"She's not here, she hasn't come home from being with her NEW boyfriend" Joie answered sarcastically.

"I'm not leaving until she comes to the door!" he exclaimed.

"Well I can call the cops and tell them I have a trespasser" she announced in her most secure tone of voice yet.

"Erin isn't going to be with anyone but me! And you can take that to the bank" he yelled again.

"I'm calling the police~so you better leave" Joie yelled back.

He tried to push his way in. Joie started to lean into the door. I ran as fast as I could for the door too. Sam yelled for me to stop. I blocked him out because now it was my turn to do something.

I heaved my shoulder into the door as he narrowly got his hand out before we slammed it shut. Joie quickly locked it. We both leaned up against the door with our backs and felt each vibration of the door as he pounded it repeatedly with his fists.

"Why aren't you calling the cops?" I asked the both of them.

"Cause he'll go away" Erin said with a hollow tone.

Sam called for me. I walked into the bathroom, and the sound of Michael's pounding diminished for but a moment.

"If I were you, I'd take Joie and leave Erin to figure this out with him. She has a problem with the love and anger too~" he said.

"What is with you? I mean, you keep bringing that up and I know it's your way of telling me how to save her without really telling me. What am I missing?" I demanded.

"You're misunderstanding what I'm really telling you-you don't realize the consequences of lack of control" he countered.

It made no sense. Any of it. Here I was, a very logical person, full of metaphors myself, yet couldn't see the forest thru the trees, so to speak.

"Listen to me," I started to argue "I am not going to leave here tomorrow and have it be 'end of story' for anyone. You've never lost anyone so you don't know the innate mortal feelings that come from being in my position. She's too young and has too much life left in her!" He stopped me...

"You're wrong. And on more than one count. It will be the 'end of story' because all you were given were seven days to say goodbye. You've spent many great moments here and come tomorrow night at 8:12pm, you will be leaving or I will take you back the second you haven't left the apartment! And don't judge me and the emotions I have, that you know nothing of" he said as if he'd had some emotions tucked deep down.

"I have to leave at 8:12pm?" I asked as I swallowed that lump in my throat again.

"If you leave any later, then you and Michael will cross paths and it will change so many things. More than you even know," he explained in an almost sympathetic tone.

I stood there looking in the mirror. Sam's demeanor had changed. He didn't look like the same angel who had sent me here a week ago. I couldn't figure it out. I knew I was missing the obvious. As hard as it was, I had no choice but to at least agree to his plan, so that I could stay until the very last second tomorrow night.

I had just barely unlocked the door when the bobsy twins had just put their hands up in the air to knock.

"Who were you talking to?" they asked in unison, looking at me like I was nuts.

"You wouldn't believe me anyway" I said, not caring anymore.

As I walked out, they both dashed for the toilet. I began to laugh and some of Sam's words of reality drifted to a place that I dare not go.

Joie had to be at work by six, so we left at five to grab some dinner. The cab driver had a Mexican radio station on and Erin and Joie began singing in the most horrible Mexican accents I had ever heard.

"You two need voice lessons-really" I shouted above them.

"You know I'm gonna start a rock band and be rich" Joie shouted above the music.

I looked out the window and actually prayed for a miracle. I even whispered to Sam, wherever he was: "I have come too far, to go back empty handed."

No reply. Exactly what I had expected.

There was a Taco Bell right down the street from the club. So I found it fitting to eat there seeing as how the cab driver had set the mood anyway.

Dinner consisted of a lot of tacos, nachos and burritos. The two divas had eyes that were bigger than their stomachs and consequently left me with the remainder of our Mexican fiesta.

Joie's laughter couldn't have been any sweeter music to my ears. I found myself memorizing everything about her mannerisms that I had forgotten over the last fifteen years.

As I watched her eat, I did recall the annoying habit of scraping her teeth on the fork. She may as well put her nails on the chalkboard. It was a very screechy sound. One that I had truly forgotten.

Joie was on the schedule until 2am and I tried to get her to get off earlier. I wanted the last hours to be mine, not anyone's but mine.

She told me that she could 'see', but since she was the "star" (Erin laughed) she had to be there.

We left Taco Bell and began to walk up the road to Memories. How ironic that my last night with her would be spent in a place ironically named just that.

Erin was unusually quiet as we walked. Joie tried to start a conversation with her.

"It won't be like this forever, you know" Joie said.

"He is crazy, there's no telling what he'll do" she said while looking away.

"Maybe he'll meet someone new, move somewhere else for a long, long time" Joie said without hesitation.

It seemed weird hearing all those words. They were both right in an eerie way. It just made me feel like I had a pit the size of an orange, in my throat.

"I wish I could hit him!" I interrupted.

"He'd hit you right back, he doesn't care" Erin said.

"What kind of guy would do that? I mean look at his family" I stopped.

I had slipped. I had really met his mother at the trial. She was nice. We sat with one another every day of the trial. I had learned a lot about his family. All of his brothers and sisters were doctors and lawyers. He was the only screw up.

"What did you say?" They both asked.

"I mean, he must come from a bad family" I said, trying to avoid a confrontation with either of them over this.

"He actually has a decent family. He's just so far into drugs and alcohol, that it now controls him" Erin admitted.

It controls him. Love and hate. It made sense, somewhat. He love the drugs and alcohol. He hated himself. They had turned him into something he really wasn't. But how could that apply to me?

"You're onto something Dawn, but you're looking at what everyone else would see and not what it really controls" Sam said to only me.

I couldn't see him. I only heard him.

We had just arrived at the club when Erin got a phone call.

Joie and I grabbed a booth and just talked.

"I want you to know that I have had a wonderful week" I said quietly.

"Me too…We have done some crazy things, huh?" She said laughing.

"Promise me that no matter where we go in life or how far apart life may keep us~ we won't forget this moment" I asked.

Her face changed and it appeared as if a light had gone on in the basement of her brain.

"You sick or something?" she joked.

"What?" I asked puzzled.

"You talk to me like you're leaving for a long time or you're going to die or something"

"Naw, just wanted to tell you thanks for a wonderful week. Don't be so serious. Besides, only the good die young. And between you and me, I've got a while yet" I fecetiously said to change the subject.

Erin came back to our table and sat down. She said that her boyfriend Greg was on his way over so that Erin wouldn't have to worry about Michael for the evening. I think we were all relieved.

As the music on the jukebox changed from one song to the next, Joie grabbed Erin and said "Let's go dance".

"Sweet Child O' Mine" by Guns-n-Roses came on. Even I couldn't resist. Now keep in mind that dancing wasn't my thing. I have no sense of rhythm, which is ironic, considering I am a musician.

We all danced on the floor by the jukebox to that old song. Erin and Joie played air guitar and sang. Poor little rock star, still waiting for her off key rock band!

Joie and Erin found all my "Saturday Night Fever" moves too embarrassing to keep dancing with me. They shoved me away and expected me to get the hint. I was laughing as I walked back to the booth. Greg was sitting there waiting for Erin. He greeted me and we started talking. I noticed that he had brought Erin some chocolate.

The song finished and they both came and sat down. As Erin reached for the Hershey bar and started to unwrap it—a distant memory came flooding back.

"Joie, did you ever tell Erin about our first Hershey bar?" I prodded.

She started to think. "You know, I don't think she has ever heard that one" she said as she started laughing.

"Well this will make you guys look at Hershey bars in a whole new way" I said.

I proceeded to tell the story of when we were four and two and our folks had just divorced and we were spending the weekend with our dad. On Sunday morning, he had slept in and left Joie and I to our Sunday morning cartoons.

Well our dad is famous for having a sweet tooth and we began to hunt for a Hershey bar. We searched high and low. It wasn't until I got a brilliant idea from one of my only childhood epiphanies and grabbed a chair and climbed on top of the counter and opened a top cupboard.

There it was. In all it's one pound glory. I pulled it down by the silver lining and Joie and I sat on the floor and ate every last bite of it.

A couple of hours later, our dad took us home. On that Monday, we were way too sick to go to the daycare. Our mom was really furious. She called our dad to yell at him for feeding us food that made us sick. He had no idea why were so sick. He explained to my mom that he had eaten the exact same things as us and he was just fine.

She told him we had diarrhea, we were throwing up etc. She was just plain mad at him.

By Wednesday we were actually feeling better and it was the day that my dad had called my mom to check on us.

Apparently, my dad had found the culprit. He had gone to the cupboard to get his "medicine" for the restroom and it was gone.

Would you believe I had managed to find a one pound slab of chocolate covered ex-lax? Boy my dad was busted.

I couldn't read at that age, and I only recognized the Hershey bar by it's trademark silver wrapper. We ate it all. Dad was laughing his butt off, but our mom sure wasn't. She failed to see the humor in it.

By now, Greg, Erin and Joie had tears coming out of their eyes and none of them could stop laughing.

"Only you Joie, only you." Erin laughed.

"It wasn't me, it was Dawn~she gave it to me" Joie responded.

"Oh come on Joie, you begged for more when the box was gone" I jousted.

We all had a great laugh at mine and Joie's expense. Joie got up and excused herself to go and start her shift. I looked at my watch when she walked away. I was beginning to count the hours now.

Time does fly when you're having fun. Even when you're not. It was almost ten when Sam showed up.

"Listen, about tomorrow~" he said.

I became silent. I hadn't really thought about "tomorrow" because of how deep it was going to cut me.

"You'll need to be out by 8:12pm, but I can't take you until shortly thereafter. You will have to find a place to meet me. Where do you want to go?" He said in a tone that left me no choice.

"I haven't really thought about it Sam. I didn't know there was a procedure." I answered.

"Well normally, this is where the story has been messed up by the time frame" he said.

"What does that mean? Someone else has done this? And they didn't leave?" I demanded.

"You misunderstood me" He quickly replied.

"I don't think I did, Sam…Now tell me what that meant!" I asked.

He just looked at me like I had hit the nail on the head.

"I was wondering something Sam" I paused

"What?" he replied.

"How do you control the two emotions" I pried.

If you could have seen him—he was aghast. Not a word. He just left. Without so much as an answer to my question. He did utter the words "Between 9:04 and 9:13 pm", but that was all he said. I knew there was something behind his metaphor. He did know something about Love and Hate. I just had to figure out what though.

Joie came back about every twenty-five minutes to get a sip of soda and charm the crowd that was now at our table.

As the night grew later-I had a dozen new memories that I hadn't had before. Somehow sleep tonite would not be a welcomed guest.

Joie came back earlier than I had expected and said we could leave now. Well, don't ask me twice. I was ready. We caught a cab back to her apartment and talked about Sunday. She was off work and she wanted to sleep in. I don't think so Jo…Not on my watch.

We got into the apartment and popped in another viewing of "Girls Just Wanna Have Fun". I could never grow tired of that movie. For that matter, neither could Joie. Her favorite part was the scene where Sarah Jessica was dancing and rehearsing with her on screen boyfriend to the song, "I Can Fly".

That song takes me back every time I hear it. As Joie started to fall asleep, I quickly plucked a strand of hair from my head. Without hesitation, I started to tickle her nostrils with the hair. You should have seen her. Sticking her fingers up her nose in her sleep to scratch it. I was laughing so hard.

She finally woke up and just slapped me. Bam! Well, you know what happened next. I started chasing her and threw her on the couch and put her in a head-lock.

"I give up! I give up!" she screamed through her tears of laughter.

I got off the couch and ran to the kitchen for a late night snack. It was 1:30 am and the clock was ticking so loud. Every second was slipping from me and I wanted so much to tell her everything.

As the microwave finished cooking the cheese on the generic version of Taco Bell's nachos, she walked into the kitchen. I grabbed her and told her "I love you Jo."

She pushed away and ask me why I was the weirdest sister on the planet.

"Sometimes you can be a real pain in the wazuuka" I retorted.

We ate two servings of nachos and then Joie started yawning.

"I'm going to hit the sack~" she said as she went to bed.

Day 7

For not being a morning person, Joie was one today. I woke up right after I slapped my face in my sleep with shaving cream on my hand. She thinks she's so clever. Go figure.

I got up and headed for the bathroom, walked in and slammed the door shut. The water was warm and I began rinsing my face. In the mirror I could see the hopeless look written all over me.

"You'll never get thru the day looking like that" Sam said.

I ignored him, hoping he'd go away.

"I'll see you tonite-be out by 8:12 Dawn. You promised" he said as he faded.

I jumped in the shower and got ready for what would be the fastest, shortest, happiest and saddest day of my life for the second time. Everything was in slow motion when I showered. My thoughts were slow and my words were gone.

I turned off the water and dried off. I smelled the towels one more time. I opened the medicine chest and grabbed her perfume. I covered myself in it. At least I could go back with her scent. Not that it would possibly ease my pain, but it might comfort me thru it.

I was dressed and about to go into the front room when my emotions got the best of me. I dropped to the toilet and began throwing up. Joie heard me and asked me what I had put on the nachos…Very funny. I laughed through my aching and somehow overcame that moment. Well, that and a swig of pepto and I was fine.

Joie wanted me to cook breakfast and of course I happily obliged. Besides, I don't think Joie ever had ever opened a cook book and used it. It was a good thing for her that they had Taco Bell and McDonald's to cook her food for her.

I asked her to peel the potatoes and you could tell immediately that that's not what divas do. Hideous I tell you. Reluctantly, she opened the drawer of silverware, grabbed the peeler and started peeling.

One thing about Joie is that she hates manual labor. Yes, even peeling potatoes is beneath her. But everyone needs humility. Even a diva who was born normal and then converted to the ways of the rich and famous.

"I'm really proud of you Jo" I said, trying to start a conversation while she peeled.

"For what?" she laughed

"For how funny you are, how talented you are at dancing and how gifted you are at peeling those potatoes!" I winked.

"Well thanks" she said as she snagged another piece of bacon.

I was putting oil in the pan for the potatoes and dumping them in when she burst into laughter.

"What is so funny?"

"Remember the time mom asked us to babysit Brandi?" she answered.

I started to laugh. That was one of those memories that needs no recalling. It is always there. And as we both looked at each other, we laughed even harder.

"Remember how we tied her to that Joshua tree-upside down, with a pillow case over her head?" she snickered.

Man we were the worst babysitters ever. We just laughed and laughed. Oddly enough, Brandi made a full recovery from that adventure in babysitting. Joie and I were definitely products of the eighties gone bad.

Breakfast was ready and Joie was just whipping out the memories left and right. I was doing great until we got to the one about her snakes in high school. Then I lost it. Because in Joie's world, all animals should come with directions. Diva or not, she was not able to think like a snake.

Joie had come home from high school one day (while she was still attending), to find both of her pet snakes as flat as a pancake and their tongues hanging out of their mouths. They were absolutely dead. My mom told Joie that perhaps she should have given them water once in a while and these kinds of thing wouldn't happen.

Joie put her purse down and swooped them up and started dipping their heads in a bowl of water, yelling "Drink! Drink!". Can you just see those two dead snakes with their tongues hanging out of their mouths and under water? That was so funny.

But wait-Joie didn't stop there. In the midst of her emergency procedures, she started CPR. What an idiot. She actually put her mouth the snakes heads and blew air into their mouths to give them her bad breath-fresh air. That alone would kill them again! They inflated like the party favors you blow into on New Year's. This girl was one amazing paramedic.

After she realized the snakes were really gone, she took it to the outer limits. Would you believe that she called up the pet shop where she bought them and demanded her money back? Yeah, the nerve of some people.

Oh—and the kicker was when she got fired from McDonalds for calling in and trying to use her "bereavement" days. Really. They wouldn't give it to her, stating that snakes didn't fall into that category of immediate family and to get her tail into work. She told them to take their job and to shove it. Needless to say, her career was shortlived at Mickey D's. The rest of us suffered be because we would not be getting any more free salads!

Joie ate the last of the bacon and I was joking on my potatoes from laughing too much.

"We have had the funniest life!" she exclaimed.

"We really have Jo~we really have." I agreed. `

I started to clear the table and Joie started to fast forward the "Girls Just Wanna Have Fun" movie to the part where Janie (Sarah Jessica) was dancing to "I Can Fly".

She turned it up pretty loud and asked me to come help her "fly"…You should have seen us. She would run and jump and I tried several times to lift her over my head and hold her up as she arched her back and put her arms out. We fell about four times. By the last try, I nailed it. We did that a few more times and I thought we could take our act on the road, until she started singing. No way…Poor little rock star-never gonna find her off key rock band.

I tossed her down and told her to quit singing. She looked around the room and grabbed the remote from the couch and chucked it at me.

I ducked, but it caught my shoulder. I scanned the room for anything heavier than a pillow to throw back.

"Seriously Joie, you have got to find a better way to fight. One of these days, someone is going to find something bigger and throw it back at you" I said as I tossed one of her shoes at her head.

As she started to run after me with it in her hand, I headed for the front door. I had just flung it open when Erin was about to walk in.

"Better stop her Erin, she's about to ruin some nice shoes!" I yelled as I ran past her.

Joie stopped and asked Erin how her night had been. Erin explained that it was actually stress free and she wanted to take a nap. Erin could smell the left over aroma from breakfast and said: "I take it Dawn cooked something healthy?"

"Yeah, but I ate all the bacon" Joie said in a guilty tone.

"That figures Jo-" she said as she went into the bathroom and shut the door.

As I watched Erin walk towards the bathroom, she whacked me. She threw that shoe and it caught my right ear. I turned and pushed her to the ground before she even knew what had happened. I was sitting on her stomach trying to pin her down when she bit me. I grabbed my leg in pain or disbelief and tried to punch her. She flipped me over and and now I was on the bottom with my face to the floor.

That had been the only move she could use to get me pinned down. To this day, no one can pin me like that.

As I lay there with her on my back and having her pull my legs backward in ways they don't bend, she took her hand and pulled me by my hair and lifted my head up and did something that you'd probably be aghast from. She farted on my head. I am serious. I struggled to get my face in the carpet so as not t smell it but she yanked me again by the hair so hard that my head lifted up and she used her other hand to fan the smell.

"Smell it! Smell it!" she yelled…

That was it…I was so mad. You don't fart on me and think I am going to just lay there and take it. Signature move or not…I got one leg free and kneed her in the back and grabbed her arms and got up and dragged her by her hair to the sink.

I turned on the water and grabbed the little hose from the sink and put her head over the drain and pulled the trigger…She was screaming so hard that Erin came out to see what was going on. As I was drenching her and her hair, Erin busted out laughing.

"Now that's funny!" she exclaimed

Joie yelled for Erin to come and help her, but Erin said no way. She told Joie that this was between her and I. That was a smart thing to say, seeing as how I was bigger than the both of them and could have taken her down as well.

After about two minutes, Joie called a truce. I was a little bit leary, because Joie wasn't the type to give up unless she got the last laugh. Skeptical, I let go of the trigger on the hose. She got up slowly and cautiously. We watched each other for about three seconds and then Joie grabbed me by the hair pulled as hard as she could.

As I was on the kitchen floor, all I could do was laugh. I told Joie to let go so that we could actually do something productive.

She slowly let go because Erin grabbed her hand and peeled her fingers apart and gave me the chance to break free. I stood up and went in the living room and sat on the couch and turned off "Girls Just Wanna Have Fun"…I turned on the radio and found a great George Michael song: "Praying For Time".

Those lyrics were so deep today. How do you pray for time, when time is in constant motion? You are always getting time as it rolls on. It's actually stupid to ask for it because it's all around us. The song talks about needing more time to get it together. Shouldn't we always be living as if this is the last go around? Yes.

Sam entered the room and I went into another. He followed me. I just didn't want to talk to him right then.

"I know you don't want to see me or hear me, but I just wanted to tell you that I truly do know how you feel." he began to say.

"You can't possibly understand any of this." I said.

"You asked me earlier, if I knew how to control the two emotions, Love and Hate"…he continued "But I never gave you an answer".

"What?" I asked, sounding puzzled.

"I didn't know how to control them…until…"

Joie had just pushed open the door and he faded.

"Come back. Sam? Come back…What does that mean?" I exclaimed.

Joie walked in and just looked at me.

"Who are you talking to" she asked as she grabbed her lifelong teddy bear…"Him?"

At that moment I had no choice but to say yes…

"He won't talk to you, he only talks to me" she said as she adjusted his tie on his red suit.

That was probably true. And teddy was going to be the only eye witness tonite and the only one to see her alive for the last time.

That bear had been thru the trial and was taken into custody for evidence. To this day, I have always wondered what he saw. And now tonite, he was going to be the only one with her when she died.

Joie asked me what time I wanted to leave for the airport.

"Leave?" I said

"Yeah, so you can catch your flight tonite" she said sarcastically.

"I can take a cab Jo-it's no problem" I answered.

"You sure? I would feel bad if you got lost or something" she said.

"Joie, only you could get lost in a cab." I said in retaliation.

She failed to see the humor in that. But it was true. Joie had no sense of direction. Even if the cab driver was driving, she would manage to direct him off course. It was for that reason that she never got her drivers license.

I made mention of the video needing to be returned. I asked Joie if she wanted to walk with me to return it.

"That's like a mile away!" she shrieked.

"And you're feet are broken? We don't need a cab!" I commented.

Well that was like pulling teeth, but she ended up going anyway because of Erin's bidding. Thank goodness for peer pressure.

I rewound the tape and we left.

It was slightly warmer even though there was snow on the ground. I just wanted to walk with her and talk about anything. My thoughts were racing and I wanted to warn her. I knew that Sam was lingering somewhere in the atmosphere and would most certainly do something to me if I broke the rules.

"You know that life is full of choices, don't you Joie?" I asked, starting a conversation.

"Is that supposed to mean something to me?" she answered.

"No, I just think that sometimes in life, our choices choose our path and once we are on that path, we think we can't get off" I explained.

"So my choices are bad?" she questioned.

"Not just yours, but everyone's. We all make choices that drastically change the outcome of things. Just to ease our pain." I continued.

"So what have I done to make my life so bad?" she pressed.

"It's not any one thing. It's a combination of decisions that have affected others around you. I am guilty of it too" I admitted.

"What have you done that was soooo crazy?" she joked

"I have tried to break some rules and have been reminded of severe consequences. Choices that I have never been faced with before" I replied.

"I thought your biggest dilemma is what new soda to try" she shouted while laughing.

"That might be funny, if I wasn't trying to tell you something" I said more firmly.

"Don't Dawn"…Sam said…

He was now walking beside me and Joie couldn't even feel him. I walked faster to avoid him and Joie started to walk slower.

"Why are you walking faster?" she said as she caught her breath.

"Come on…Keep up" I said without explanation.

We all but jogged the last quarter mile to the video store. And when I looked back, he was gone. I hate it when he does that.

She yelled at me and said we were calling a cab to go back. Great idea. Sam deserves a free ride anyway.

The cab showed up and Joie told him to crank the heater. The radio was playing that song "More Than Words" by Extreme. I started humming it when Joie broke in and told me to stop singing to their song because she didn't like them anymore.

"Why do you say things like that?" I asked.

"Because Erin and I were on their tour bus one time and they got really mad when I chucked their George Michael Tape" she said without thinking.

"Well I would be mad too…I'd kick you off the bus!" I laughed.

"Well, we don't like them anymore…They couldn't even take a joke" she finished.

So she asked the cab driver to change the station. Well by the time he did that, we were back at her place.

She paid the cab driver and we went in and I plopped on the couch. Erin was taking a nap on the futon and I turned the T.V. on but kept the volume low. I looked at my watch. It was a little after three. No calls from the caller and no sign of Michael…yet…

It was a really mellow afternoon. Kind of like the calm before the biggest storm you could ever hope to endure. I just couldn't stop feeling sick to my stomach. I kept going to the bathroom.

Joie finally asked me why I was so sick.

"Did you put 'Drano' in our food?" she said snickering…

"Ha, ha…No, I just have an upset stomach" I answered trying not to laugh at her witty comment.

Joie flipped the channel to Mtv. She loved all those hard rock bands. I failed to see their musical talents while screaming into a microphone. As I was complaining about the music being ridiculous, a new video by Firehouse came on. I actually liked those guys. It was called "Spend My Life"…Ironic, to say the least.

Erin woke up because of Joie's beautiful singing. I quickly turned it up so as to drown out that poor little rock star who still hasn't found her off key rock band.

Erin laughed as I drowned Joie's vocals out. I smiled because all I could see were her lips moving and no more sound. It was a great moment in music history.

Joie asked Erin what the plan was for the evening and I felt like throwing up again. So I dashed to the bathroom.

"I thought we'd leave about seven and head over to pick up Greg and the girls" Erin explained.

They both walked over and watched me in the bathroom.

"If you're contagious, you better where a mask or something" Erin said.

"No, better yet, she can put a bag over her head!" Joie laughed.

"I'm fine, really..." I said, rinsing my mouth out and flushing the toilet.

I wandered into the kitchen and looked in the fridge. Nothing but cold pizza in there. Joie and Erin could live off that stuff if it were the only thing on earth to eat. I however, have to have variety. As long as it's not pizza or seafood, I can handle it.

There was some frozen chicken in the freezer and I asked Joie and Erin if they'd eat some dinner with me before they left and I left.

You don't have to ask Joie twice when it comes to chicken. She loves it. Especially fried chicken. So I got it out and threw it in the microwave to start thawing. I decided to make baked potatoes for dinner instead of asking the diva to peel them again so that we could have had mashed potatoes, I didn't want to hear the complaining.

While the chicken was thawing, I asked Joie to open her Christmas present.

"Are you sure, it's not even Christmas." she said, trying to be funny.

"Really, open it...I want you to see it before I go" I said.

She tore into the wrapping paper. I wish that moment could have been frozen. She lit up from an obvious very happy flashback in our childhood.

"Lincoln Logs!!!" she shouted happily. "They are perfect...I can play with these for hours on end!!" she finished.

She leaned toward me to hug me and I was really glad that she liked them. As she let go of me, we laughed and recalled all those Friday nights ago when we had built so many towns for so many people. To be a kid again, would be wonderful.

She dumped all the Lincoln logs on the floor and asked me to join her. Erin must have thought we were idiots, sitting on the floor playing together like kids. Joie thanked me again and again…

Just then the beeper went off on the microwave for the chicken. I jumped up and washed my hands before I touched the slimy chicken. I hate touching chicken. I asked Joie if they had any sandwich bags. She motioned to the second drawer down. Unopened, they were in there. I had to laugh. Did these two use anything in the kitchen?

I opened the box of bags and grabbed two. I put them on my hands and started fixing the chicken. I heated the oil to a reasonable temperature and carefully dropped the breaded chicken in the oil. It began cooking and browning. I poked some holes in the potatoes and tossed them in the microwave.

"What vegetable do you want to have as a side dish Jo?" I asked.

As I looked in the cupboard, I knew she'd say corn. That was all they had in there.

"Well corn, I guess" She responded…

"Good choice" I laughed.

The chicken started smelling quite delicious. Joie came in and started to pick at a piece that was on the plate about to go in the oven to stay warm. I smacked her hands and told her to wait. She smacked me in the back of the head. Rather than start a wrestling match right then and there, I opted to set the table.

Erin came in and said she'd be glad to do it, since I was doing the cooking. Funny how Joie never thought to offer her services. That's what a diva does.

While Erin set the table, Joie asked me if I was going to go and pack my things. I stood there. I really didn't want to, because it meant the time was getting closer. She insisted I go into her room and pick up my things. She came into the kitchen and put her hands on my back and began to guide me to her room.

I walked in and stopped.

There on top of my empty suitcase was the Elvis box. She stood in the doorway waiting for me to pick it up.

I swallowed the next biggest lump I'd ever felt, and reached out to pick it up. She was telling me to open it. I didn't want to. I silently read those words again…

ॐ

To Dawn,

Please take care of this. It was not cheap and it's a collector's item. You break this and you die.

Take care, it's been a banner year…

Your Sis,

Jo

I turned to her and tears were in my eyes, but I didn't want to blink. I couldn't cry. It wouldn't be right.

"I love it Jo–" I said as I kept the tears from falling.

"But you don't know what it is…Open it!!" she said looking at my eyes.

I opened the box, already knowing what was inside. But this time, it had a whole new dimension attached to it. She was with me. My tiny dancer in my hand. Softening the blow that was yet to come, by giving me that gift tonite.

It was Elvis in front of a pink Cadillac in front of the gates of Graceland, painted onto a plate.

"It's registered and numbered" she said, sounding extremely happy.

It really was a collector's item. Not because it had come from the Bradford exchange, but because she wouldn't be here for this Christmas or anymore for that matter. That plate took on an infinite worth at that very moment.

I knew that no matter where I went in life, that plate would go with me. And I would cherish every glance I had of it. Why? Because my sister had taken the time to give me a gift that would far exceed it's own personal value. And you can't buy that kind of worth. You just can't.

I was about to blink and knew the tears would fall, when Erin yelled that the chicken was burning. Saved by the bell. Joie ran out to go turn the chicken over.

I smiled as I closed the box and laid it back in the corner, by the rest of the gifts she wouldn't be sending home.

Dinner was just about ready when the phone rang. It was our mom. Joie talked to her for a minute and told her that they were going out that night and she'd call her later.

"Love you more" she said as she hung up for what would be the last time with her.

As we sat down for dinner, I knew that my dad would be calling in a bit. Everything was falling into place. Except my soul. I was changing. My stomach wasn't so much queasy from the events yet to unfold as it was scared and didn't want to leave her alone.

We ate dinner and Joie talked about how great the food was. I ate slowly, even though time refused to stand still. And wouldn't you know, that Sam was nowhere to be found.

As I drifted off to another place, I tried to make some sense of what he told me. He admitted to having trouble with 'Love and Hate'…But what did that mean? He was so vague.

Like clockwork, the phone rang for Joie again. It was our family in Az. She talked for a few minutes and said she had to go and get ready. Seeing this all unfold now, made me believe that someone had a hand in her saying goodbye to all of us in our own ways. Yet, we would have said so many things differently to her, if we had known how everything was going to change on Dec. 3, 1990.

Isn't that the truth. Our vision is always clearer once we've gone thru it and have time to look back at it.

We finished dinner and just tossed the dishes into the sink. I didn't feel like washing them anyway.

Joie got some old photos out and we went through her book of memories. Funny how everything this week was about to become a blur again. I wanted to bring something back that would help me deal with what lay ahead.

Joie's photo album had pictures from when she danced with the Arizona Stars. We laughed at how young she looked. In the background on some shots were our brothers and sister. They were young. To me anyway. To her, that were exactly the right age.

She kept smiling when Brian's pictures popped up. He was a cutie. How could you not want to squish his cheeks?

"Remember when we used to dress him up in all the department stores" Joie recalled.

"I do…He was so hard to put in all those cute suits!!" I half heartedly laughed.

I looked at the clock. It was close to seven now.

Erin was in the bathroom getting ready when the phone rang. I made a run for it.

"Hello?" I said

Nothing. Not even breathing. Just a click and that was it.

I started to get mad at the caller. Joie came in and said that it wasn't him.

"How do you know?" I asked.

"He would have said something." she said instintively.

Erin made a quick comment that it was probably Michael acting like an idiot and that she wasn't scared, because Greg would be there shortly and they would be going out so as to not have to be confronted by Michael.

Joie asked me if I'd iron her skirt.

I couldn't bring myself to do it.

"It's just ironing, Dawn" she said trying to make me feel guilty.

"Fine, I'll do it"…I said in protest.

I didn't want to iron the clothes she'd be wearing when Michael came.

As the iron got hot, Greg knocked on the door. Erin yelled for him to come in.

Erin told Joie to hurry up because they were leaving.

"Oh, go ahead you two, I'll catch up with you later" Joie said to the both of them.

"You're not going over with us?" Erin asked

"No, I will meet you there" she said as she walked towards Erin.

They hugged and Erin was about to walk out the door when she turned around and said: "See you later Jo"

"See you later Erin"…Joie replied as the front door shut.

I stood there and realized that it was the last time they would ever speak. I finished her skirt and gave it to her. She put it on and started doing her hair and make-up…

It was 7:40 and I was getting sick again.

I unplugged the iron and put it back on the shelf.

I heard Joie turn on the blow dryer and start to do her hair. I stood in the hallway looking into the bathroom. She was leaning to her left with her long hair hanging down and scrunching it as she dried it. Her signature look.

I walked down the hallway and noticed the Christmas presents again. I bent down and picked up my Elvis plate and touched the loving words she had written on the front of the box. The tears started to form again.

I quickly put the box back and started to panic. I can't do this. I am going to have a heart attack. My chest was hurting. The second hand on the kitchen clock got louder with each tick.

Joie came out with partially wet hair and looked at me and smiled…

"Did you call the cab?" she asked

"I was going to do that right now" I answered…

"Here, let me call them"…she walked towards the phone. She picked it up and dialed the cab company we had been using all week. As she hung up she turned to me and said "They're on their way"…And she walked down the hall back into the bathroom…

I grabbed my things and got really nervous. I just couldn't think straight. I couldn't think about anything but stalling. I knew that Sam was close by.

Within a couple of minutes, the cab driver honked.

I went down the hall to say goodbye.

This was it.

This would be the last time I would see her or hear her laughter. So many things to try and remember.

My heart was bleeding.

She walked towards me and I grabbed her. I pulled her close to me and wrapped my arms around her...I didn't say anything...I just kept swallowing.

"Dawn, you're squashing me" she said in her muffled tone.

"I love you Joie! I have always loved you!" I said with my voice quivering...

"Thanks for coming...Thanks for a great week" She said as she pulled away...

I had her hands in mine and just stared at her...For that split second, our eyes met and she looked like she was ok with everything. It was if she knew and she was telling me she was going to be ok...

The cab driver honked again.

Joie opened the front door and let me out.

My feet were like lead. I couldn't make them move.

I kept my eyes on her until I turned the corner and went through the gates and into the cab. As I got in, I saw her peek through the curtains. She waved at me and I blew her a kiss.

The cab driver left. He had no idea how badly my soul had just been torn. We had only driven a few miles when I had looked at my watch. It was about ten after eight.

I yelled for him to stop. He asked why...

"Just stop!" I screamed.

He did.

I gave him some money and got out...

🍁   🍁   🍁

Michael knocked on the front door and just walked in. Joie heard the door open and assumed it was Erin. So it took her a few minutes to come out of the bathroom.

When she did, she yelled at Michael and told him to leave…

"Where is Erin?" he demanded.

"She's not here, she's out with Greg!" she yelled back…"Now get out!!"

🍁   🍁   🍁

I began to run back to her apartment. It was cold. It was really hard to run in the cold.

I had left my jacket in the cab.

None of that mattered now.

None of it.

I had to save her.

🍁   🍁   🍁

Michael wouldn't leave.

Joie tried to get him to leave, but he refused. So she just ignored him and finished getting ready.

He began to look around the apartment. He was looking for some sort of a weapon now. Something to hurt her with.

I ran hard and fast. My memories were the only things sustaining my long run back to her.

As I realized what was happening to her, I cried out so desperately. I was so hollow. So angry. So sad.

Michael had found a blunt object and walked to the bedroom where Joie was matching her shirt with her skirt.

He hit her in the back of the head with it and she started to fall to the ground.

I was calling out to her now…

"Joie! Joie!…I am coming…Hang on!" I yelled as I ran faster.

My lungs were burning. I couldn't think about anything but her pain. My legs were not keeping up with my mind.

I stopped in the middle of the street and threw up…I couldn't breathe…

Joie was semi-conscious and started to defend herself. She scratched Michael several times but he kept hitting her.

She screamed out for him to leave. He was in a rage now. He couldn't stop.

She cried for anyone to help her…Anyone…

✤   ✤   ✤

I was about a half a mile away now…My tears were burning my eyes. My lungs were aching for warm air…

I kept calling her name. I kept running…I could only see our whole week together just flashing thru my mind at speeds that I couldn't even see.

It was her perfume on my clothes that sustained me now…

✤   ✤   ✤

Michael had Joie unconscious now. She had stopped screaming.

He went into the bathroom and found the blow dryer…

✤   ✤   ✤

I was losing my strength. I knew she was fading fast. I had to run faster.

My body couldn't run that last few hundred yards…

I was yelling for help for her. I yelled to the heavens to stop this agony.

I had to throw up again…Something was trying to stop me.

I screamed out to Sam to leave me alone as I pushed my body to the limits I had never pushed it before.

I was running without pain now…I had blocked it out.

✤   ✤   ✤

Michael took that last bit of life from her as he strangled her with the blow dryer and the pot-pourri pot cords.

She had passed out. He held on to the cords until all signs of life were gone from her body…

He quickly wrote "The Caller" on a piece of paper, lay it on her stomach and closed the front door and left.

I was almost there. I was going to save her. I was going to bring her home.

It's Christmas. I believe in miracles.

As I got up to her apartment complex, I saw Michael leaving. I didn't have time to go after him.

I ran those last few yards to her door yelling for help…Anyone…

Nobody heard me. I got to the front door and grabbed the handle.

I turned it so as to go in…

The door wouldn't open!!!

The knob was turning, but the door wouldn't open!

I began beating on the door and screaming for Joie…

"JOIE!! JOIE!! I'm here. I can't get in. Hang on"

He was there…He was on the other side of my eternity. He was holding the door closed with one finger.

I kept pushing and pushing. Nothing was moving. Nothing. She was slipping away. It had been more than 4 minutes since Michael had left.

I heard him yell from the other side of the door.

"Dawn…You can't do this…Go back!!" Sam said as he held the door shut with just one finger.

"You let me in Sam!! You let me in!" I said as I cried harder than I had ever cried.

"You don't understand Dawn…You will be the first." He yelled…"I can't let you do this…You will be the first"

I was sobbing beyond belief as I kept pushing the door…I was begging, pleading and trying to make any kind of deal…

"Sam, she's not going to make it…LET ME IN!!" I yelled with more anguish than I ever knew was in me…

I started to fight harder…I threw my whole body into the door…

"I know what you must be feeling…I was there too!" He said…

"Let me in!!I want her back!!…Please Sam!! Please!!" I begged

"None of us have made it past this point…You have got to make it…We have to see what it's like after this!" he said as he held the door…

I was weeping and shaking…I couldn't get the door open…I started to slide down the front of it…Crying tears of such sorrow…

"Dawn, I was like you once. Someone gave me this chance and I blew it. I tried to save the love of my life and we both died" He finally admitted.

'Sam! Let me in! I have to save her. She needs air…" I said as I sat in a slump on the ground by the front door.

"Don't you see Dawn, I was like you too but now I am in this state and can never go back! You have to make it. We have all felt like this and we don't know what comes after this part of the journey! I am not even with the woman I love!! I can't let go of this door! You are the one who has to make it!" He said now sobbing

I couldn't believe my ears. He had been like me…He had known all along what my feelings were…

I just sat there shaking at the thought that she was truly gone now…And then it happened…

I heard a click…

The door opened, just a crack…I turned and fell into the entryway. There he was…A man who had done the same thing but had failed.

I stood up. I looked at him as a person now…

He had tears in his eyes.

"None of us have made it…We all tried to change our endings, but failed. I had to hold the door shut so we could see you go back and find out what happens when you let history be as it should" He said, now crying.

"Who was she Sam?" I asked, now caring about his pain.

"Lisa was the one person who really knew me and when she died in that car wreck, I couldn't forgive myself for getting out earlier that night…So when they came and asked me if I wanted to have 'Seven Days To Say Goodbye', I jumped at the chance of saving her." he explained now crying like a child.

"What went wrong?" I asked, wiping the tears from my face and his.

"Everything…I didn't have the faith to know that it would be ok. I was so selfish in my pain that I changed everything that night…and so you see, I had to hold that door shut. I want to know what happens after you say goodbye" he looked up at me.

"I don't know what happens." I shrugged and turning my thoughts to my sister.

It was silent now. I prepared myself for what was about to become a really painful moment.

Sam had given me something that I was willing to steal from myself. My next moment in time with her.

My shaking turned to just being cold from my running. My tears were no longer freezing on my face, but rolling down my cheeks. I turned and started down the hallway.

I walked in the room and it was dark. But there she was, beautiful and quiet. I could see her and wanted to reach out and hold her.

As I did, she started to fade.

"Don't take me yet Sam," I begged. "I want to be by her for a moment"

He just stood there with a look that, for that split second, told me I had an extra moment with her.

I tried to hold her, but couldn't touch her. I was leaving now. I just lay my head on the floor next to her.

I began to weep again. I could tell she was gone. We just lay there on the floor like we were falling asleep one last time together.

I sat up and leaned over her forehead and kissed her goodbye.

Sam told me it was time.

"How come you haven't seen Lisa, Sam?"

"I broke the rules. I have to suffer the consequences of not being able to control 'Love and Hate'" he said as the moment grew silent.

"But…" I started to say

"I loved her so much that I had hated who I became without her and it consumed me. I didn't want to live and have her be gone. So when they asked me if I wanted the chance, I took it and blew it" He said with regret in his voice.

"I wanted to save Joie, and I would have if you hadn't of held the door" I admitted.

"But you have to go back. Because none us were given the opportunity to go back in time after our loved ones had been gone for fifteen years. Our grief was so fresh when they offered us the chance, that we all blew it." he continued "I picked you because you had come all these years without her and I knew you would be able to go back and not alter anything" he said.

"But I am going back now with a fresh pain that wasn't there before" I softly said, "So who is better off now, you or me?" I finished.

"We might just be the same" he replied as he guided me down the hall.

We were the same, he and I. He might have been better than me since he put my growth first. He stopped me from doing what everyone else wanted to do and allowed me to now see the story as it was written from that day forward.

We walked down her hallway and into......

🍁   🍁   🍁

Saturday, Dec. 3, 2005.

I sat on Joie's grave for the 15th anniversary of her untimely death...Sam was there, and asked me how the last fifteen years had felt.

"It's been hard not having her around, but I know there's a plan" I explained.

"Is there anything you'd do differently?" He asked.

"I have to say that I wouldn't change anything in my past to make my future unfold some other way." I answered, now understanding what he really meant.

🍁   🍁   🍁

Sam left that day and took with him the experience of Seven Days To Say Goodbye. In the journey that I had completed, he learned of how a story can only have one ending once it's been played out. It's not for anyone to change nor deviate from the destiny that awaits all of us.

❧   ❧   ❧

My fifteen years without her have become a part of my everyday life. She's not forgotten, but she's not a part of this life anymore. I can't include her as if she were here, because she can't be two places at once .Thus, I am living this life here without her for but a moment, so that I can again, catch up with her in her life when we get reunited on the other side. And it is there, where we will never have to say goodbye again.

About the Author

Dawn Michele writes her first novel based on her own personal experience of life, death and what happens after we are left here when we lose a loved one. Residing in Greensboro, North Carolina she intends on moving to Nashville to pursue her songwriting dreams.

978-0-595-39127-1
0-595-39127-3

Printed in the United States
53953LVS00003B/193